'You've [...]
arrogan [...]

'Is it conce [...] el?'
Marcus cha [...] try it some
time, Hayle [...] nonest, I mean. Then
perhaps we might get somewhere.'

Hayley licked dry lips. 'And where is it that you
want to get, Mr Maury? With me, I mean. Isn't
one string to your bow enough?'

'Perhaps. But it would need to be the right
string to strike the desired chord.'

Dear Reader

With the worst of winter now over, are your thoughts turning to your summer holiday? But for those months in between, why not let Mills & Boon transport you to another world? This month, there's so much to choose from—bask in the magic of Mauritius or perhaps you'd prefer Paris... an ideal city for lovers! Alternatively, maybe you'd enjoy a seductive Spanish hero—featured in one of our latest Euromances and sure to set every heart pounding just that little bit faster!

The Editor

Shirley Kemp was born in South Wales, but has the blood of all four countries of the United Kingdom in her veins. That fact probably explains her infuriatingly impulsive and restless personality, which has recently taken her off to live in France. Second eldest in a family of seven children, she found that spare time was rare, but she read voraciously and wrote for enjoyment. Writing romantic fiction is a natural extension of that youthful pursuit and she still enjoys it just as much.

WHEN STRANGERS MEET

BY

SHIRLEY KEMP

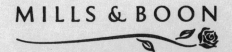

MILLS & BOON

MILLS & BOON LIMITED
ETON HOUSE, 18-24 PARADISE ROAD
RICHMOND, SURREY TW9 1SR

*First published in Great Britain 1994
by Mills & Boon Limited*

© Shirley Kemp 1994

*Australian copyright 1994
Philippine copyright 1994
This edition 1994*

ISBN 0 263 78495 9

*Set in Times Roman 10 on 11 pt.
01-9405-55429 C*

Made and printed in Great Britain

CHAPTER ONE

OH, NO! Frank Heaton. Of all the bad luck.

Hayley Morgan stared aghast into the next compartment of the train, unable to believe her eyes as the rather tubby man came striding in her direction, the one person in the world she had hoped she would never have to see again.

Instinctively, she ducked down into her seat, wishing she had a magazine or something to hide behind, but all she carried was a small handbag into which she couldn't even pretend to delve.

Perhaps he hadn't seen her, she thought a little wildly. Perhaps it was coincidence that he seemed to be heading in her direction. She watched him indecisively for a moment, praying he would find a seat without having to continue along the train. But he came on, making for the connecting door into her compartment.

She gritted her small white teeth against a sudden surge of fury. It was bad enough being hounded out of her job by the unwanted and blatantly sexual attentions of her boss's son, without this chance meeting with him on her train to freedom.

She tossed her thick dark hair in a gesture of defiance and her velvet-brown eyes glinted, unnaturally hard.

There was no way she was going to put up with his gropings and innuendoes now she had given up her job as his father's secretary. But past experience of Frank Heaton's rhinoceros-thick hide had taught her that even the strongest resistance might not be successful against his thrusting ego, and she certainly didn't relish making a scene in public. She shuddered at the thought of en-

6 WHEN STRANGERS MEET

during more of the humiliating indignities that had
plagued her life for the past year. Frank Heaton seemed
incapable of understanding that anyone could find him
unattractive, let alone repulsive.

She jumped to her feet. If he hadn't seen her already,
he would as soon as he stepped into the half-empty compartment, but she might still be able to take evasive
action.

There was no time to manoeuvre her case down from
the rack. She'd had enough problems getting it up there.
Her slim form and slender arms weren't meant for wres-
tling heavy cases on to racks placed conveniently for
giants. But it was no use fretting; she would have to come
back for it later. The main thing was to find somewhere
to hide.

Frank was actually opening the door as Hayley sped
up the long, open compartment, sighing with relief as
she remembered the loo. He could hardly force his way
in there. Her sigh turned to a groan as she tried the
handle and found the door locked.

With her heart beating rapidly in near panic, she
rushed on to the next compartment, which was first-class,
and hesitated. It was empty, except for one lone man.
If Frank came here, he would spot her at once. But,
since she couldn't go back, she would have to go on.

The man was sitting in the seat nearest the aisle, and
Hayley slowed down, smoothing her skirt over trim hips,
hoping to look at least a little dignified as she passed,
but she needn't have bothered—he was fast asleep, with
his head to the side and his long legs extended beneath
the little table before him.

Looking back through the dividing glass door, she saw
Frank's head, unmistakable with its thinning hair
combed across his narrow brow. His round black eyes
seemed fixed determinedly in her direction, and her heart
sank. There seemed little doubt now that he was actively
looking for her.

It went against the grain to give up, but it looked as though she might have to... unless...

Almost without thinking, she ducked under the table where the sleeping man sat, and moved up into the window seat alongside him, hoping that the table-top and the man's large frame might offer some kind of screening.

The stranger's face was turned towards her, his expression one of total relaxation, completely oblivious of the drama going on around him. He was very handsome, she noted with a kind of detached interest, with a strong, lean face, firm chin and well-shaped lips, slightly parted to reveal the gleam of white teeth. In addition, he was well built, beautifully dressed, and his thick reddish-brown hair was immaculate even in sleep.

She gave a grim little laugh. If he woke now to find her here, what would he think? What would he say?

Well, she would soon find out, she thought as she heard Frank's heavy tread approaching with a tremor of dread. How she hated that man, who had hounded her until she had almost been a nervous wreck. There had to be some way of avoiding this unpleasant idiot.

The stranger stirred, and, acting on her second uncharacteristic impulse of the day, Hayley leaned forward and kissed him, so lightly that their lips barely touched, tilting her head, letting the thick curtain of her dark brown hair fall forward to help shield her face.

'I say, have you...? Oh, I'm sorry... I didn't realise you were—er...'

Hayley heard Frank's mutter and his cough of embarrassment as he hurried by, and gave a relieved little smile, her lips moving softly against the stranger's in a silent prayer. She'd closed her eyes to avoid seeing Frank's face if it should loom at her, and opened them cautiously as his heavy footsteps died away.

Warily, she raised her lids, and gave a startled gasp. For bewildering seconds her senses swam in the depths of eyes more intensely blue than any she had ever seen. She was brought back to earth by the realisation that there was ice as well as colour in the hard glare.

'May I ask what you think you're doing?' The deep pleasant-timbred voice was heavily uncompromising.

She'd half expected amusement, or plain surprise, so was completely thrown by the glare of icy dislike he shot at her.

She felt a swift rush of embarrassment, quickly followed by resentment.

'Nothing very terrible, if I were a man.' She glared back at him, meeting the hard look with scorn. They could dish it out, she thought grimly, but obviously couldn't take it. 'Men steal kisses all the time, don't they?'

'Some, perhaps,' he conceded coldly. 'But I don't happen to be one of them.'

'No?' She studied the handsome face, the arrogant tilt of the head. A powerful man, used no doubt to deference—and to being the one to make the passes. With a grim little laugh she said. 'I don't suppose you *need* to stoop to that.'

'Correct!' He smiled grimly. 'You, on the other hand, obviously do.'

Hayley felt her colour rising. Her hatred of Frank Heaton had inevitably overflowed to men in general, but for most of them the cap fitted anyway. This stranger, being handsome and, she had to admit, with a strong masculine presence, had probably never had to try too hard. But, like all the others, he would if he had to.

'There was a reason for that,' she said stiffly. 'I was desperate and just had to do what was necessary in the circumstances.'

'Desperate? For a kiss?' His brows rose tauntingly. 'I find that hard to believe.'

He stared into her wide velvet-brown eyes, presently fixed with renewed antagonism on his hard face. His expression was easily recognisable, though it didn't quite constitute a leer.

He went on cuttingly, 'Although, if you go around throwing yourself at every available man, I can see how it might deter one or two.'

His gaze swept almost insultingly over her pale oval face, framed in thick, curling dark hair, with its straight little nose and wide mobile mouth, and down, apparently missing nothing of her trim figure and firm, shapely bosom.

'I don't. Throw myself at men, that is.' Hayley cut explosively into his assessment. 'This is the first time I've ever done it...in an emergency.' She added sarcastically, 'If it's any consolation, I didn't enjoy it.'

'That does compensate a little.' The grim features hadn't relaxed one bit. 'What kind of emergency?'

Hayley, meeting his scornful gaze, sensed he wasn't prepared to give an inch... This handsome stranger with the icy, unsmiling eyes obviously had a heart of stone. Why should she bother to explain? The story wasn't a pretty one, and he wasn't exactly the confiding type. And besides, he was the enemy.

'It's a long story,' she said flatly. 'I wouldn't want to bore you with it.'

'Try me!' he insisted, dangerously civil. It sounded more like a command than a request. 'I might find it riveting.'

But it was Hayley's eyes that were riveted...on a balding dark head that was bobbing back again in her direction. Tenacious as ever, Frank obviously hadn't given up the search.

Hayley felt renewed dismay, which turned to grim determination. Neither Frank nor this arrogant stranger would be witness to her defeat.

'You won't appreciate the joke, I know,' she said with a tight little laugh. 'But I really do need to kiss you again. Would you mind?'

Without giving the stranger a chance to reply, she put her mouth over his and hung on to him grimly until the danger had passed.

When she opened her eyes again, the blue gaze wasn't just icy, it was furious.

'No wonder you didn't enjoy it, Miss Pushy. You've got a lousy technique. If you're going to do this sort of thing, then at least learn to do it well.'

Hayley's eyes blazed. 'Of course, it wouldn't be your technique that's lousy.'

'I'll let you be the judge of that.'

Without warning, he caught her against him, his mouth descending forcefully on hers.

Taken unawares, Hayley had no time to summon her resistance. The first touch of his lips brought a shudder of dread that had her struggling like a small creature in a trap. Desperation churned at her insides, giving her almost superhuman strength as she dragged herself away from him.

She was breathing as though the whole world lacked oxygen, and her brown eyes were wide with panic.

He stared at her in consternation. 'What is it? An asthma attack or something?' He still held on to her arms, but his fingers relaxed their steely grip a little.

Dragging air into her lungs, she managed to say hoarsely, 'No. Just the kind of attack I might have expected from someone like you.'

His mouth drew into a thin, hard line. 'And what's that supposed to mean?'

'What it always means,' she said bitterly. 'That men never miss an opportunity to show the *weaker* sex just how strong and overpowering they can be when they want something.'

'A moment ago, it was *you* who wanted something.'

She gave a short, harsh laugh. 'Yes. But not what you think.'

The corner of his mouth curled contemptuously. 'Tell me, my little dark-haired gypsy—what was I thinking?' He drew her closer. 'Can those big, soft pansy eyes really see into my mind?'

'No. Any more than your ice chips can read mine.'

He nodded. 'True. But I can take a guess.'

Without warning, his hand went up to grasp the nape of her neck, his long, strong fingers lacing into her hair. Slowly he brought her face to his, smiling thinly at the flicker of fear that showed in her gaze as his mouth hovered above hers.

'Relax, Miss Pushy. This isn't going to hurt a bit.'

Hayley began to struggle, but his arms closed about her, holding her, to her surprise, with a gentle strength that miraculously soothed her raw nerves. How the miracle was achieved, she didn't know; she was only aware of a strange warmth creeping through her tense body, relaxing muscles tautened for battle, until she lay still against him.

His lifted his head a little to murmur, 'That's better.'

Slowly his lips began to move against the unprepared softness of her own, but with a thoroughness that caused an explosion of feelings, impossible to control or to describe, but which left her breathless and faintly dizzy.

When at last he released her there was a hint of amusement in the cold blue eyes.

'Get the idea?' he queried, with a mocking lift of thick brown eyebrows. 'Or would you like a little further practice? In my opinion you need it.'

She stared at him, speechless, until her erratic heartbeat subsided and she could swallow the peculiar lump in her throat.

Why hadn't she felt the same loathing and contempt she had come to anticipate when a male mouth forced itself on to hers? Where were the stirrings of nausea Frank Heaton's hot, wet mouth had always engendered?

For looks and physique you couldn't compare this stranger with the Frank Heatons of the world, she reasoned grimly, but it all boiled down to the same thing in the end: overwhelming male conceit.

'You really do think you're God's gift, don't you?' she gritted. 'Well, thanks for the offer, but once was more than enough.'

His face assumed an air of disappointment. 'And I thought I was doing you a favour.'

She laughed mirthlessly. 'Fortunately you'll never know how big a favour.'

'Really? Then perhaps we're still not quite quits.'

His eyes rested pointedly on her lips, an unexpectedly smoky look in the blue depths. It seemed any minute he would be repeating that kiss.

Hayley recoiled. It was a man's world, she thought bitterly, a world full of socially acceptable chauvinism. But his kiss had stirred some hidden depths and, as much as she hated the fact, she wasn't sure she could withhold a response this time either, which was galling in a way he'd never understand.

She gave an exasperated sigh. In trying to avoid one man's unwelcome attentions, she seemed to have laid herself open to something even more disturbing. It was time to make another escape.

She ducked quickly under the table and came up in the aisle.

She said scornfully, 'I've appreciated your help. But I hope we never meet again.'

'Believe me, Miss Pushy, I echo your hope.' The blue eyes narrowed intently, without even a trace of humour to soften his expression. 'But stranger things have happened.'

Back in the corridor, Hayley hung about outside the loo, just in case Frank came back and she had to dive inside, but there was no sign of him and, gradually, she began to breath normally again.

Her legs felt weak, but she had a feeling it was less the result of unexpectedly seeing Frank as the onslaught she had suffered from the stranger—as disturbing, in its own way, as any of Frank's efforts.

Thankfully, they would be in Paddington shortly, so she would soon have to make a move to recover her luggage—if it hadn't been stolen, that was.

After a while longer she went cautiously back into her original compartment. With relief, she saw her case was still on the rack where she'd left it.

With a bit of luck Anthea would be on the platform waiting, so she wouldn't have to hang about once she got off the train.

Her spirits lifted as Anthea's bright yellow hair became clearly visible among the waiting crowd.

'Hayley! Hayley!' Anthea called, waving excitedly. 'Over here!'

'I know. I can see you.' Hayley wagged her finger in a quieting gesture. 'Not so loud.'

She looked furtively about, but there was no sign of Frank.

With a sigh of relief she rushed over and grasped Anthea's arm. 'Quick. Let's get out of here.'

'What's the rush?'

'No time for questions and answers,' Hayley said hurriedly. 'I'll explain later.'

But Anthea was transfixed. 'Oh, look! There's Felicity Braun.'

'*The* Felicity Braun?' Hayley cast a curious look about the station platform. 'Where?'

'There!' Anthea squeaked with excitement. 'Look! There!'

Hayley's gaze followed her friend's pointing finger. It really was Felicity Braun, she confirmed, with a little spurt of interest. She must have come to meet someone off the train. The actress was spreading her arms to embrace a tall man with reddish-brown hair and an attractively muscular frame, apparent even in his conservative but obviously expensive suit.

'And that hunk must be her latest!' Anthea exclaimed, adding ecstatically, 'Oh, isn't he gorgeous?'

The 'hunk' pulled back a little, and Hayley saw his face. With a gasp of surprise, she realised that the man with his arms about the beautiful young actress was none other than her obliging stranger.

Out here, in the open, he was even more devastating. His lithe body simply oozed sex appeal, making it difficult for her to tear her eyes away. She had a moment of wry satisfaction as she remembered that last kiss. Not many could say they'd been kissed passionately by Felicity Braun's latest. She couldn't help wondering how Felicity would feel about that.

'It's all a question of taste,' she said unenthusiastically.

Anthea giggled. 'Well, he certainly suits my taste. Give me half a chance...'

'But he wouldn't, would he?' Hayley said sharply. 'He's a man.'

'Since when have you become a man-hater?'

Hayley groaned. 'Don't ask. Then it can't depress you.'

Anthea shot her a curious glance, before her eyes returned to the couple, who were now trying to extricate themselves from the crowd that had begun to gather around the actress.

'Come on. Let's go,' Hayley said impatiently.

At that moment the man looked in her direction, holding her startled gaze with an enigmatic look from those piercing blue eyes. He raised his brows briefly, issuing, it seemed to Hayley, a mocking challenge, before turning his attention back to his companion.

Hayley felt as though an electric current had been passed through her body, making her shudder.

'He was looking straight at you.' Anthea, whose sharp eyes missed nothing, was staring in amazement at Hayley. 'Do you know him?'

Hayley gave what she hoped was a nonchalant shrug. 'A passing acquaintance,' she said lightly, though, for some reason, her heart was beating madly against her ribs.

As Anthea's mouth opened for further questions, Hayley grabbed her arm firmly. 'Let's get out of here, before I meet up with another acquaintance who *won't* be so keen to pass.'

But, strangely, the recent past and Frank Heaton had been overshadowed. It was the stranger's face she saw as she settled into the passenger seat of Anthea's creaky old Mini, and that last wry lifting of his brows seemed to pose a strangely intriguing question she would never now be called upon to answer.

Anthea's flat was a reflection of herself, chaotic but fun, and Hayley breathed a sigh of relief when they were safely inside.

'I can't tell you how good it is to be here,' she said gratefully as she sank down on to the gaily coloured settee. 'Are you sure you don't mind me staying for a while?'

'Mind? I'm delighted.' Anthea, who had somehow miraculously conjured up a cup of tea in the tiny cluttered kitchen, handed one to Hayley and sat down beside her to sip her own. 'Strange as it may seem, I've really missed you. I still can't understand why you didn't come up here with me in the first place.'

Hayley sighed. 'I know. I wish now that I had. But at the time I was enjoying my job, and I'm not at all sure I'm really a city-type girl.'

'Fair enough.' Anthea shrugged. 'So! What happened to make you suddenly change your mind? Was it a man?'

'Sort of. But not in the way you mean.' Hayley gave a short laugh. 'Unless you call sexual harassment romantic.'

Anthea grimaced. 'I call it a damned nuisance, but I wouldn't have thought *you'd* be beaten by it.'

'I wasn't *beaten*,' Hayley replied defensively. 'Just sickened. Especially when it was condoned by a man whom I'd previously respected...my boss...but unfortunately also father to a hatefully odious son.' She shuddered with remembered distaste, and then shrugged. 'I don't suppose you could entirely blame Mr Heaton Senior for defending the reputation of his son and heir against the word of a mere secretary.'

'So you gave up?' Her friend scowled. 'Hayley Morgan! Where's your fighting spirit?'

'Still intact.' Hayley laughed at her ferocity. 'But, for once, I overrode it with a little common sense. Since old Mr Heaton had a heart attack he's been training his son Frank to take over the reins, so I wouldn't have stayed on to be Junior's secretary anyway. But also, with Frank more or less in control, the business has started to decline quite badly, and there's a rumour it's in the process of being sold. All in all, not a very good bet for my future.'

Anthea frowned. 'No. I suppose not. Still...it goes against the grain to know the pig got away with it.'

Hayley's chest began to heave as the fury she'd deliberately buried began to push up again to the surface.

'Don't remind me. I still have dreams in which I'm murdering him.'

'Nightmares?' Anthea queried sympathetically.

'No. They're good dreams.' Hayley grinned. 'I always wake up feeling better afterwards.'

They giggled together, renewing their former closeness.

There was a small silence, and then Hayley said, 'As a matter of fact Frank was on the train coming up, but I managed to avoid him.'

'Good for you,' Anthea approved. 'How did you manage it?'

Hayley grinned, surprised that she could think about it now without becoming angry.

'By making love to a strange man.'

It was said to shock, and Hayley wasn't disappointed by Anthea's reaction.

Her eyes flew open. 'What? You made love on the train?'

Hayley laughed. 'Not exactly. But I did kiss him. Twice.'

'You did?' Anthea's eyes danced delightedly. 'Tell me more. What did he do?'

'He kissed me back.'

'And then?'

'Frank disappeared and so did I.'

'Oh!' Anthea's expressive face fell. 'Was that all there was to it?'

Hayley shrugged. 'More or less.'

'He didn't even try to make a date?'

'Anthea!' Hayley cried reprovingly. 'It's that kind of attitude that encourages men to think the way they do. Besides, do I look like the type who would let herself be picked up by a stranger?'

Unperturbed, Anthea grinned. 'No. But he might at least have *tried*.'

'He might have, but he wouldn't have got anywhere.'

'Why not? Was he ugly?'

'No.' Hayley's eyes twinkled with sudden mischief. Now it was all behind her, she could afford a little joke. 'In fact he looked just like Felicity Braun's latest.'

She waited to see how long it would be before the penny dropped. She didn't have long to wait.

'The "passing acquaintance"!' Anthea gasped. 'It was him, wasn't it?'

Hayley nodded.

Anthea's eyebrows seemed in danger of shooting off her face. 'You kissed him? I mean…he kissed you? And you let him get away?'

'He wasn't running far. Only into the waiting arms of another woman. Your beloved Felicity Braun. Poor woman! Probably completely oblivious to the reality of the man.' Hayley snorted contemptuously. 'So typical of the male of the species.'

Anthea frowned. 'You didn't used to be so bitter.'

'Do you mean I haven't had cause?' Hayley demanded, serious again. 'After my experiences with Heaton Junior, I'll be giving men a very wide berth.'

'I say that all the time,' her friend sighed. 'But I still fall in love with the next pair of sexy eyes I see.'

'Well, I certainly won't be,' Hayley said positively, pushing aside a vision of cold but fascinating blue eyes that were definitely sexy. 'Men are the kind of trouble I can do without.'

Anthea said, 'Hmm.'

They sat for a while, each wrapped in silence and their own personal thoughts.

Then Hayley heaved a sigh and spread her hands dramatically. 'So here I am, trying out pastures new, and on the look-out for a job that's both interesting and financially rewarding. Let's hope it won't be long in coming.'

'Amen to that,' Anthea drawled.

'And amen to the hope that any males thereabout will view me with complete uninterest.'

Anthea laughed derisively. 'What a hope! With your looks? If I had them, I might be willing to put up with one or two office gropers.'

'You wouldn't, you know,' Hayley cut in forcefully. 'There's nothing more horrible than being mauled by a pair of podgy hands, being kissed unexpectedly by moist blood-red lips! Ugh!'

She gave a deep shudder of revulsion, and Anthea patted her hand sympathetically.

'Sounds rough,' she said, for once entirely serious, an expression she could never hold for long, and soon she grinned. 'But never mind! Look on the bright side. There couldn't be two like Junior.'

Hayley looked aghast. 'Ye gods! I hope not!'

Anthea's grin widened. 'Then let's say double amen to that.'

Hayley's spirits rose. It had always been good to be around Anthea and she had a feeling that, from now on, by way of a change, things were going to go her way.

She looked forward to making a new start, and knew she would have to do her best to forget the last few months, but the situation had bitten deep, leaving scars that would heal only as time passed and her confidence returned.

She might joke about it, but it would be a long time before she would be able to forget the humiliation. Old Mr Heaton had unexpectedly added to her agony when she'd been driven at last to ask for his protection from his son. He'd hurt her deeply by hinting that she might have been more than half to blame for Frank's objectionable behaviour, muttering something about short skirts and tight sweaters being a deliberate provocation these days.

Since Hayley had always dressed circumspectly and had never worn either garment to the office, she'd felt justified in arguing against the implication, but Mr Heaton had dismissed her words with impatience.

In the end she'd had no option but to leave the job she'd once enjoyed and which she'd had since leaving secretarial college four years ago.

Later, in Anthea's bright little guest room, Hayley stared at herself in the full-length mirror, her gaze moving critically over the slim lines of the body Frank had seemed unable to keep his hands off.

The skirt she wore wasn't short, but it couldn't help but follow the curves of her shapely figure. The fitted blouse, too, faithfully outlined the firmly rounded bosom. There was no denying she looked youthful and attractive, she thought ruefully. But for the past year that attractiveness had been more of a curse than a blessing.

Hayley sighed. There wasn't too much she could do about her shape, unfortunately. But she could do something about her attitude towards men in the office, which from now on, she vowed, would be nothing short of repressive.

But first of all, of course, she had to find a job.

CHAPTER TWO

WHICH was easier said than done.

More than a week later, with no sign of a job in the offing, Hayley sat disconsolately in Anthea's kitchen, sipping at her third cup of tea. With so much time on her hands, she thought gloomily, she was turning into a tea-aholic.

Despite having done the rounds of agencies as well as writing off in answer to countless advertisements for secretaries, she'd had only two interviews, neither of which had been successful.

Since Heaton's was the one and only job she'd had, she supposed her experience might seem a little lacking to anyone who didn't know she'd run the office practically single-handedly in terms of administration.

'Any luck?' Anthea came breezing in just after six o'clock, sniffing appreciatively at the stew Hayley had simmering on the stove, having taken on the job of cooking to relieve the boredom.

'No. Nothing in the mail and nothing doing at the agency. The word "secretary" seems to have been outmoded by, "Multi-lingual SuperSec with thorough knowledge of every known make under the sun of computer",' Hayley grumbled. 'No wonder no one's bothered to acknowledge my modest curriculum vitae, where my only claim to other languages is a B in O level French. Why choose a non-starter when you can have SuperSec?'

'Rhubarb! You'd run rings around the best of them.' Anthea slumped down at the table, kicked off her shoes, and put her sturdy legs up on another chair. 'Where you

fall down is in being too honest and a darned sight too
modest. You've got to try a little flannel.'

She picked up the newspaper in which Hayley had been
searching for vacancies and began turning the pages.
'Look! Here's one! If you want a taste of the glam and
the glitz of being a top sec, it's right up your street.'

Hayley peered at the black-edged box Anthea was
stabbing with a blood-red fingernail. It read:

> Temporary position: Personal secretary urgently re-
> quired by managing director of national engineering
> company. Must be competent, organised, self-
> motivated.

Daytime and evening telephone numbers were given
with the address underneath.

'A temporary job to cut your city teeth on,' Anthea
suggested drily. 'No mention there of languages or computer wizardry. And you've worked in engineering for
years.'

Hayley laughed. 'You can hardly compare Heaton
Engineering with a *national* company.'

And then, as Anthea opened her mouth for a pungent
reply, she said hurriedly, 'Don't say it. I'll ring first thing
in the morning. And I'll tell them I'm the best thing
since the wheel.'

'The ad says *urgently*,' Anthea remarked irritably.
'With daytime and evening telephone numbers given,
that's got to mean *very* urgent.' She pointed into the
hall. 'There's the telephone. What are you waiting for?'

The response to Hayley's telephone call was im-
mediate. A man answered and, after taking brief par-
ticulars—name, address and a short outline of her
experience—he gave her an appointment for the following morning at ten o'clock.

'Thank you.' Hayley's head swam a little with the
speed of it. 'Who shall I ask for?'

'My name's Marcus Maury.' The voice was deep and faintly husky, and sent a strange little tingle up Hayley's spine. 'Just ask for me at Reception.'

Hayley put the phone down, still in a bit of a daze. Marcus Maury. She repeated the name with a frown. Somewhere, in the far reaches of her brain, the name seemed familiar. But, try as she might, she couldn't make the link.

But an evasive memory was the last thing on her mind as she waited the following morning in the empty outer office of the managing director's suite.

She'd had a restless night of anticipation, waking with a headache, and was wearing the tinted glasses she sometimes used for very close work. She'd worn them in the office at Heaton's when Frank was around, in the hope of deterring him, but it hadn't worked. Studying their effect this morning, however, she thought they made her look a little more intellectual, and decided to keep them on for the interview.

Out of sheer nervousness, she'd got on the wrong bus, and felt as though she'd done a round tour of London before finding another to take her in the right direction. The bright sunshine and the cheerful bustle of the streets would have enchanted her on any other day, but she'd been hot and flustered by the time she'd arrived fifteen minutes late. She'd introduced herself rather breathlessly to the young receptionist, who, obviously expecting her, had rung through to announce her arrival and then showed her up into the empty and rather opulent office of Mrs Audrey Blake, the name beautifully inscribed on a steel nameplate on the immaculate desk. If this was the secretary's office, Hayley mused, what must the inner sanctum be like?

She hadn't long to wait to find out. A tall man appeared briefly in the doorway and beckoned her to enter.

Hayley rose a little unsteadily on her unaccustomed high heels. They made her look taller and comple-

mented her shapely legs, but she wondered now if they
hadn't been a mistake. She'd chosen her outfit carefully.
In deference to the fact that Maury's was a London-
based national company, she'd decided on the most
sophisticated outfit in her sparse wardrobe, a well-cut
jade-green suit with paler matching blouse, its tie front
demurely knotted at her throat.

Her thick dark brown, naturally curly hair had been
pulled back into an well-ordered coil at the nape of her
slender neck, and unconsciously her hand went up to
check for stray ends before she made her entrance.

She was halfway across the large, thickly carpeted
office before her eyes focused clearly on the man seated
behind the gleaming desk.

'Come in, Miss—er—Morgan,' he said in answer to
her rather diffident good morning. 'I shan't keep you a
moment.'

She wanted to apologise for being late, but he seemed
to be intimidatingly busy, and somehow she didn't have
the nerve to interrupt.

His head was down as he finished writing in his diary,
and with a sudden, gut-wrenching start Hayley recognised the rich red-brown tint of the thick hair before the
blue eyes rose to confront her.

She had trouble stifling her shocked gasp, but he
seemed not to notice her reaction.

'Well. Thank you for being punctual.' He indicated,
with a wave of his lean hand, a chair placed opposite.
'Won't you take a seat?'

It was somehow amusing that, after all the rush and
haste and anxiety, he hadn't even noticed she'd been late.
Not that it mattered now.

With a sinking feeling, Hayley sat. So much for things
going her way, she thought morosely. Of all the people
in the world he could have been, Mr Marcus Maury had
to be her stranger. If he recognised her, he gave no sign
of it. Perhaps the glasses, smart outfit and severe hair-

style would be camouflage enough to carry her through, she thought hopefully. After all, he didn't know her name, and they had met only the once in totally different circumstances.

At the moment he looked like a man with a lot of more pressing things on his mind than a quirky meeting on a train and a few stolen kisses.

'As you may have noticed, we're a little disorganised at the moment. My personal secretary has unfortunately had an accident, leaving me a little high and dry.' He grunted irritably. 'Fell off her blasted horse. Not her fault, of course, but damnably inconvenient.'

'Yes, I'm sure,' Hayley murmured, despite herself amused by his vehemence. With a touch of irony she added, 'Some secretaries can be indispensable.'

But he wasn't paying attention. He went on frowning for a moment longer, his thoughts obviously unhappy, and then he seemed to give himself a mental shake.

He straightened, turning his blue gaze full on her for the first time since she'd entered the room, and her heart missed a beat as she waited for the inevitable flash of recognition. It wasn't long in coming.

'I've got this damned important meeting this morning, and nobody capable——' He cut off sharply, staring at her with a puzzled frown between his brows. 'Haven't I seen you somewhere before?'

Hayley bit her lip, wondering if she should brazen it out or jog his memory. If she didn't, it was possible he might not remember exactly where they'd met. But it would only be a respite. He was bound to remember sooner or later.

'We met on the train,' she said flatly, offering no further prompt to his memory.

The frown deepened and then lifted in sudden enlightenment.

'Well, if it isn't Miss Pushy,' he drawled, with a slow shake of his head. 'I didn't think coincidence could stretch so far, so soon.'

'Neither did I,' Hayley agreed gloomily. 'But it just about fits the pattern of my luck and the way its been running lately.' She sighed. 'By the way, my name's not Pushy, it's Morgan. Hayley Morgan. You have a note of it just there.'

She pointed an irritable finger at his notepad.

The thin smile was cold, self-assured, his glance sweeping over her face in a slow, searching look.

'You know,' he said slowly, after some seconds, 'the disguise almost had me fooled.'

For an instant Hayley battled against a feeling of hopelessness that she should even try to get the better of this man. Then her courage reasserted itself. What had she to lose now by standing up for herself?

'It isn't a disguise,' she argued heatedly, because the accusation wasn't true. Or at least, only after a fact. 'How could I possibly know Marcus Maury would turn out to be you?'

He grimaced wryly. 'You mean you didn't recognise me on the train?'

She was genuinely puzzled. 'On the train? Why on earth should I?'

She stared at him, remembering that his name had seemed familiar, but, though she studied him carefully, his face was the face of a stranger. If she ever had seen him before, with those distinctive features, she was sure she would have remembered.

'I'm not a city girl, in fact just a country bumpkin.' Her mouth curled. 'If you're famous or something, I wouldn't know.'

'Prominent, perhaps, rather than famous.' He seemed unperturbed by her contempt. 'But certainly quite well known.'

'But not well known enough, unfortunately, to reach my former humble domain,' Hayley sniped at his arrogance. 'I hope that doesn't hurt your feelings too much.'

He said drily, 'I'll survive.'

The interview wasn't going at all well, Hayley realised with some misgiving, but she wasn't about to give up without a fight. 'However, I don't think this has much to do with anything. I'm offering you my services as secretary, not myself.'

'No, of course not,' he intoned mockingly. 'That you keep for strange men travelling on public transport.'

Hayley's face flamed, but she kept her voice steady. 'That was the result of an unforeseen emergency, as I told you.'

He nodded. 'But you haven't explained the emergency.'

'And I'm not going to.' Hayley was dimly aware that the situation was getting out of hand, but somehow she seemed bent on self-destruction.

'Because you can't find an explanation that's feasible?' He gave her a measured look.

Red-faced, Hayley retorted, 'No. Because it's none of your damned business.'

He seemed perfectly calm. 'I think your behaviour rather made it my business.'

'And I disagree.'

Blue eyes locked into velvet-brown in silent struggle, neither seeming willing to give way. They'd obviously reached a stalemate.

Hayley's breath was short and sharp, her feelings more of dismay than anger. There seemed little to salvage now but her pride.

'I don't think there's much point in my staying, do you, Mr Maury?' she said with dignity. 'You probably have others to interview, so I won't take up any more of your time.'

She stood up a little shakily, but this time it wasn't the shoes that made the ground beneath her feet feel unsafe.

He sighed and leaned back in his chair. Making a pyramid of his fingers, he placed the tips against his firm chin.

'I haven't, as a matter of fact. That is, there are no others to interview. It could be something to do with the fact that the post is temporary.'

She stood woodenly before him, making no comment. With an irritable gesture he growled, 'Oh, do sit down, girl.'

Hayley sat, facing him mutely, waiting for round two of the battle which she knew she couldn't win. He held all the aces.

To her surprise he said, 'You *can* understand English, type accurately and spell correctly, I suppose?'

'Of course,' Hayley answered, lifted out of her depression by astonishment.

He gave a grim laugh. 'No "Of course" about it. I've been treated to some pretty imaginative efforts from other applicants in the past couple of days, and, quite frankly, I haven't any more time to waste.'

Hayley felt a ray of hope. Perhaps all was not yet lost. Her abilities in the areas he'd mentioned were never in doubt. 'I'd be quite happy to take a test.'

He shot a quick look at his watch, his firm lips in a tight line. 'I haven't time for that either. It'll have to be a real job of work or we might as well both forget it.'

She gave him a wary look. Was he saying what she thought he was saying? Despite a feeling that this was all too good to be true, Hayley's eyes brightened.

'And as I said, it's temporary, to last only until Audrey's well enough to come back.'

She nodded. 'I understand.'

Even a temporary job would be better than nothing. It would give her a chance to gain experience of working in the city and earn her some money to pay her shared expenses.

'And the salary?' she said, trying not to sound tentative. She was worth as much as she could get.

He grinned sardonically. 'Saving the most important thing till last?'

'Of course. We all have to live, Mr Maury.'

'True.'

He named a figure which took Hayley's breath away. It seemed like a fortune, until she remembered the high cost of living in London.

'Subject to satisfactory performance, that is.'

'But of course.' She managed to sound composed. 'OK. I agree.'

He stood up and came around the desk, looking down at her assessingly, his eyes moving quickly from her neatly coiled hair to her chicly clad feet. He seemed satisfied with what he saw.

'I suppose it's too much to hope that you also take shorthand.'

'I do, as a matter of fact.' Hayley couldn't help feeling a little smug. 'A hundred and twenty words a minute.'

In his prime, Mr Heaton Senior had kept her speed up with the hasty gabble he'd called dictation.

'Minutes? Verbatim?'

'If that's what you want.'

'Not entirely. Just the salient parts would do.'

It was the first time she had seen him genuinely smile, and the effect transformed his good looks to devastating. She sat transfixed by the unexpected gleam of approval in those piercing blue eyes.

'And you've no other appointments for the day?'

Bemused, Hayley shook her head. 'Not unless the agency's rung since I went out.'

'Then let's go.'

She stared at him disbelievingly. 'Don't you at least want to see my curriculum vitae? I mean . . .'

He frowned as she ground to a halt. 'You do want the job, don't you?'

'Yes, of course, but . . .'

He gave a short grunt. 'Then you've got it.'

With a sweep of his lean hand he ushered her into the outer office.

'You can work in here. I understand Audrey won't be back for quite some time. But for now I'm late for that meeting, and I need you with me. Just grab a notebook and some pencils.'

If she'd been nervous at the thought of the interview, the prospect of minuting a meeting of which she had no background knowledge terrified her. And a quick glance at the frowning profile of Marcus Maury convinced her he wasn't a man to make allowances.

Still, he was only a man, not God! she comforted herself. And she could only do her best.

And, surprisingly, doing her best didn't prove that difficult. Marcus Maury did take the time to give her a short briefing. The Maury Corporation was in the process of taking over a number of smaller companies, and this was the preliminary meeting to separate the wheat from the chaff and fine down the options.

There were ten people present in the gleaming boardroom, eight men and two women, all presumably associated in some way with the Maury Corporation. Hayley was aware of quite a few curious glances being thrown her way.

They worked through lunch, with sandwiches and tea and coffee being brought in on trolleys, but Hayley barely touched anything.

Her pencil flew over her notebook, propelled by her interest in the substance of the various reports, and it was only the light touch of Marcus Maury's hand on her shoulder and the sound of his voice calling a halt to the proceedings that brought her back to the realisation of his presence.

'There are one or two reports still to come,' he informed the meeting, sounding a little irritable. 'But the details can be circulated by post as soon as possible, to give everyone a chance to incorporate the information into their findings for the next meeting.'

Chairs scraped as people rose and a general buzz of conversation began.

'Oh, by the way——' Marcus Maury cut through the hubbub simply by raising his hand '—Audrey Blake's accident now seems likely to keep her away from the office for some time. I don't think many of you will have failed to notice my new secretary.' He indicated Hayley with a brief nod and a wry smile that had Hayley flushing faintly. What exactly had he meant by that? 'Miss—er—Hayley Morgan, who will be running things in Audrey's absence.'

She supposed, a little drily, that she should be glad he hadn't introduced her as Miss Pushy, and there was a glint in his eyes that might mean he was thinking along the same lines.

Hayley looked away swiftly, and smiled a little hesitantly at the assembly.

A murmur ran around the room and a number of people came up to introduce themselves and congratulate her.

Hayley nodded in response to their greetings. She supposed Marcus Maury had had no option but to introduce her, but it all seemed a little premature, since he hadn't yet seen the results of her work. She wasn't really concerned about that. Her work was the one area in which she was entirely confident, but that incident on the train had set up some constraint between them, and it was, she felt sure, bound to raise its embarrassing head again at some time in the future. He was a man who obviously preferred reasons to loose ends. She set her chin firmly. Well, he'd just have to accept that she had no intention of tying this one for him.

It would be humiliating, to say the least, to be reporting to him, as her new boss, all the sordid details of her unhappy experiences at the hands of her old boss ... or, at least, those of his son.

She wished fervently that he would soon forget and allow her to put the past behind her.

But if experiences could be forgotten, the effects might take a while longer.

As she stood to one side, waiting for Marcus Maury to finish the conversation he was holding with a large white-haired man whom he'd introduced as chief financial officer, a hand touched against the small of her back, startling her into an audible gasp. Heads turned as she shied away from the well-built young man who was looking down at her in amused consternation.

'Steady,' he said, removing his hand hastily at the sight of her stricken face. 'I didn't mean to frighten you to death.' He held out his hand. 'I'm Martin Lukes, up-and-coming hopeful from the lowest rungs of Finance.'

'Oh, hello!' Hayley swallowed hard, managing a smile as she put her hand into his, where, to her dismay, it trembled a little.

He gave her an understanding smile. 'Has your debut been that nerve-racking?'

Glad of the proffered excuse, she nodded her head. 'A little.'

Mentally she castigated herself. She really would have to learn not to react so violently to every unexpected touch. Heaton Junior was many miles away, and there seemed nothing of the lecher in the pleasant open face before her.

'Sorry I jumped,' she said. 'I must have been daydreaming.'

He grinned. 'Don't let the boss hear you say so. Dreams of any kind are banned during working hours. Concrete plans only are allowed.'

He glanced across the room to where Marcus Maury was looking their way.

'And, actually, at the moment he doesn't look too pleased. In fact I think he wants you.' He winked, before moving away. 'And who in his right mind wouldn't?'

Hayley bit her lip and crossed the room in answer to the imperious lift of Marcus Maury's hand.

Walking back to the office alongside him, Hayley wondered how she'd ever had the nerve to kiss him. If he'd been awake, and emitting this overwhelming air of authority, she would probably never have had the courage to do it. A peculiar tingle shot up her spine as she stole a surreptitious look at that firm, well-shaped mouth. It was incredible to remember that she had kissed him and, what was more, that he had kissed her back.

He turned and caught her gaze on him, and his brows rose questioningly.

'Is there something you want to say to me?' He halted to give her his complete attention, much to her consternation.

'No, I...' she stammered, racking her brain for inspiration. 'I just wondered how soon you wanted these minutes typed up.'

His brows rose in a faintly mocking arch. 'Well, at least you're keen, and I suppose that's a start.'

He took her arm as they turned a corner in the corridor, and she steeled herself against the warmth of his fingers through the fabric of her jacket. Anticipating the now familiar inward shudder that came in response to any man's touch, she was taken completely by surprise by a strange *frisson* of excitement, and remembered, with renewed confusion, her reaction of pleasure to his kisses on the train.

How could one man's touch be horror while another's was magic? she asked herself wonderingly, before she began to pull herself together. She'd given up one job to escape sexual harassment, and had vowed that from

now on she would give men—particularly men at work—
a very wide berth. Now here she was practically melting
at the merest touch of Marcus Maury's hand. They'd
already started off on the wrong foot in that respect and
she would need to be extremely careful if she wasn't to
give him the wrong impression and find herself in an
even more impossible situation than her last.

She edged surreptitiously away from him and, to her
relief, he dropped his hand.

She found herself sighing with relief as they turned
into the managing director's suite.

'To get back to your earlier question,' he said, pausing
in front of the secretary's desk as she took her place
behind it, 'I don't expect miracles on your first day. But
I do expect competent interpretation and accuracy of
presentation, so take the time to get it right first time.'

Hayley bit her lip. Well, if that wasn't expecting miracles, she'd like to know what was, she mused wryly.

'I think you'll find available somewhere all the
necessary stationery, office machinery, etcetera. Samples
of presentation you'll find in the filing system, if you
care to look at some back numbers of the minutes.'

'I'll manage, thanks,' Hayley said, superstitiously
crossing her fingers. She hadn't yet had time to identify
the computer, and hoped that the manual for the model
was available to hand.

'Good.' He nodded his satisfaction and turned his disconcerting eyes on her face, with a little frown between
his brows.

Hayley caught her breath, wondering what was coming
next.

To her surprise he said, 'You look a little pale. You
didn't eat much at lunch, and, from what I saw in the
boardroom, you seem a little jumpy. Are you on a diet
or something?'

She shook her head, a little embarrassed that he'd
noticed her nervy reaction to Martin Lukes. 'Pale is my

natural colour, and no, I never diet. I just wasn't hungry. The rest, I think, is probably nervous tension.'

He gave a little shrug, as though he too had been surprised by his own interest.

'Well, there is a staff tea-room along the corridor if you should feel like a snack later,' he said, walking towards his office. 'Meanwhile, if you get stuck on anything, I'll be here for an hour or two.'

The telephone rang on her desk and he picked it up, answering the caller crisply, before putting the receiver down with a snap. Hayley could see he was a man who hated to waste time on extraneous conversation, one who'd have no patience with girlish chats during working time. Not that she was prone to that sort of thing anyway, but it made her realise what would be expected of Marcus Maury's personal secretary.

'I'll put this through to my room for this afternoon,' he said. 'Normally I like my calls to be screened before anyone is put through to me, but I'll let you off for today.'

Was that real humour or a glint of irony she saw in those cool blue depths? she wondered, but she didn't have time to dwell on the thought.

Hayley couldn't believe her luck. The computer was the same as the one she'd used at Heaton's. It had a more sophisticated printer, but she should manage to work that out when the time came.

The next couple of hours passed in a haze of absorption. All of the companies under option were engineering companies, and Hayley was surprised at the number that were in financial difficulties. If they were incorporated into a larger organisation, however, perhaps there was still a chance of their survival.

The telephone rang frequently and it was a relief not to have to stop to answer it. She was startled, therefore, by the harsh sound of the buzzer, cutting through her concentration and making her heart leap uncomfortably. With fingers that shook slightly, she pressed the intercom.

'Yes, Mr Maury?' she said a little breathlessly.

'Take a break, Miss Morgan.' His voice sounded richer, deeper, over the telephone. 'Have a cup of tea or whatever in the staff-room, and bring me a coffee on your way back. Black, no sugar.'

'Yes, Mr Maury,' she said again, and put the phone down with a sigh.

Now she came to think about it, she was hungry and tired. It had been a strange day, exhilarating in a way, but exhausting. She couldn't wait to see Anthea's face when she told her about her new job and who it was she was working for. Her eyebrows probably wouldn't come down for a fortnight, Hayley thought with a grin.

The staff tea-room was almost empty. It was obviously the tail-end of the tea-break, and only two girls remained, gossiping cheerfully in the corner. They looked up as Hayley entered and regarded her curiously.

'Are you new?' one asked. She was a small, plump blonde with inquisitive blue eyes and a mischievous smile. 'I haven't seen you before, have I?'

'No,' Hayley said warily. She had a feeling she was speaking to the root of the office grapevine, and didn't think Marcus Maury would be happy with anyone who nourished it. 'I started work here today.'

'Marcus Maury's new secretary!' the girls cried in delighted unison.

'Yes,' Hayley acknowledged guardedly. She supposed there wasn't much harm in their knowing that. Everyone was bound to find out eventually.

'Well, that was quick,' the blonde said. 'Audrey's seat is hardly cold and he's filled it already.' She grimaced. 'I don't see why he couldn't have given the job to one of us.'

The other rather mousy girl giggled. 'That would have pleased her ladyship. . . I don't think.'

'She's not going to be too pleased when she hears this bit of news either.'

They stood up to leave, obviously agog to pass on their snippet of information. The blonde placed a hand on Hayley's arm and said confidentially and seemingly without rancour, 'Lucky you. He's a stunner, isn't he?' She made an assessing survey of Hayley's appearance. 'Make the most of having him to yourself. When Audrey finds out what you look like, my guess is she'll get better in a hurry.'

The mousy girl giggled. 'Nothing short of a minor miracle.'

They left, and Hayley heard them giggling all along the corridor, probably bound for the typing pool.

She had a sticky bun and a cup of tea and went to sit in the corner by the window, ruminating on what the girls had said. It was obvious that Audrey Blake wasn't too popular with some of the other girls, who seemed rather less than sympathetic at the news of her accident. Most of it was probably jealousy, since they just as obviously lusted after Marcus Maury, or at least the job as his secretary. If she was here for any length of time she would be bound to come in for her own share of catty remarks.

She took the coffee back to the office, wondering if he might have wanted a sticky bun with it. On the whole, she thought not. His hard, muscular body showed no tendency towards flab, and she guessed he would not be an admirer of junk food.

The door to her room was open and she pushed it wider, her attention on the cup of coffee and the task of making sure none of it spilled over into the saucer. She almost dropped it in surprise as the couple embracing in the room moved apart at her entrance.

By superhuman effort, she managed to steady the cup in its saucer and cover her embarrassment.

'I hope I haven't kept you waiting too long for your coffee,' she said, managing to sound unperturbed.

'Not at all.' There was not the smallest hint of embarrassment on Marcus Maury's countenance, and he didn't hurry to remove his arm from about the woman's waist as he indicated to Hayley that she should put the coffee cup on the desk. 'Could you manage to find another for Miss Braun?'

'Of course.' Hayley had recognised the young actress. She was hard to mistake, with glowing red hair and a wide gleaming smile, only slightly fixed as her gaze rested on Hayley.

'Oh, don't bother for me, Marcus, darling. I drink too much of the stuff anyway, and I haven't time to stop.' She tossed a thick tress of hair out of her eyes in an elegant gesture. 'Won't you introduce me?'

'Yes, of course. This is Hayley Morgan. She's taken over today, in lieu of Audrey Blake, who's had an accident.' To Hayley's surprise he added, 'So far quite capably, I'm relieved to say.'

To Hayley he said, 'I presume you know Miss Felicity Braun.'

Looking into the girl's assessing hazel-green eyes, Hayley thought she probably knew her rather better than he did himself. Or, at least, the actress was being very transparent at the moment. Her expression was definitely territorial and issued a subtle warning to trespassers.

'Yes, of course,' Hayley agreed with a formal little smile. 'My flatmate is a great fan of Miss Braun's.' And then, because that sounded a bit double-edged, she added hastily, 'I am too, of course.'

'Thank you.' Felicity's eyes turned glacial. 'I'm sure Marcus is very lucky to have found you to step into the breach so quickly and so efficiently. Most agency staff are notoriously inept these days.'

Ouch! That puts me in my place, Hayley thought, with a spurt of wry inner amusement. She might have disputed the agency dig, but that wasn't the point at issue, she knew. Was the jealousy personal, she wondered, or did it extend to any female who came within touching distance of Marcus Maury? Hayley was inclined to think the latter, ruminating that the job of defending that magnificent specimen of manhood against predatory females would undoubtedly be an exhausting occupation.

What a pity Hayley couldn't reassure Felicity that the actress's presence in Marcus Maury's life was far from being an annoyance. It made Hayley feel safe. At least she needn't fear being the recipient of her boss's unwanted attentions, with this vigilant lioness about.

Hayley was dismissed with that distinctive toss of the head, and moved around to sit at her desk as Felicity drew Marcus towards his office, shutting the door firmly once she'd got him inside.

Hayley was unaware it had opened again, seconds later, until she felt a hand on her shoulder.

With a muffled cry she wrenched away, turning to face him with a look of defensive anger, which quickly turned to embarrassment as she saw his astonishment.

'I... I'm sorry. For a moment I thought...'

She ground miserably to a halt.

'That I was going to attack you, judging by your reaction.'

'No. I was just surprised.' She took a deep steadying breath. 'Did you want something?'

A frown formed between his brows. 'Just my coffee.'

He reached around her to the desk to pick up his cup, and she stood there, tense and on edge.

'I didn't take you for the nervous type,' he said a little shortly. 'Relax! I'm not going to bite!'

'I'm sorry,' she apologised again. 'My first day. It's been a bit unnerving.'

He nodded and moved away with his cup. He seemed suddenly anxious to get back to his office.

'Yes. Well, don't overdo it,' he said absently. 'Perhaps you'd better store what you've done so far and go home.'

He didn't toss his hair, but it was distinctly a dismissal, Hayley noted, trying not to feel irrational annoyance. Miss Braun might not be able to stay long, but they obviously intended to make the most of the time she had available. And Hayley was definitely extra to requirements.

'Where on earth have you been?' Anthea was sitting in the kitchen with a plate of beans on toast in front of her. 'I was beginning to get really worried.'

Hayley flopped down tiredly into a seat opposite, kicked off her shoes, and stretched out her long legs.

'I've been working like a slave all day.' She eyed the beans on toast with a sigh. 'Is that all there is to eat? I'm starving.'

'So was I,' Anthea said, sounding cross. 'I hung on as long as I could in case you were bringing something in ... perhaps a pizza or ...' She stopped. 'What do you mean? Working all day? Where?'

Hayley laughed. 'You're so quick on the uptake sometimes it amazes me.'

'Skip the comedy.' Anthea pushed her plate away. 'Have you got a job? I mean, a real job?'

'It's real enough. For the time being. I've been taken on temporarily by the Maury Corporation. I'm to stand in for the managing director's secretary, who's had an accident.'

'Wow!' Anthea sat back in her seat with a stunned expression on her face. 'You're working for Marcus Maury?'

'Yes. Why? Do you know him?'

Hayley remembered Marcus Maury's disbelief that she hadn't recognised him. Perhaps he'd had a right to be surprised after all.

'I know of him. There's something about him in the papers all the time,' Anthea said. 'And I've seen photographs. He's quite nice-looking, isn't he?'

The photographs couldn't have done him that much justice, Hayley thought in amusement, otherwise Anthea would have recognised him at the station, where she'd admired him only as the latest acquisition of Felicity Braun.

For some reason, now the time had come to reveal her surprise, Hayley felt disinclined to reveal it. If nothing came of this job, maybe it would be less embarrassing if he remained a shadowy figure labelled 'boss'.

'He's not bad,' she said offhandedly. 'A bit of a perfectionist, perhaps.'

'And a slave-driver too, by the sound of it!' Anthea said critically, adding firmly, 'Well, if you're sensible you'll begin as you mean to go on and let him see you don't intend to be put upon.'

Hayley laughed. 'I'll try. At the moment I'm too busy trying to keep my head above water to be bothered with planned strategies.'

'Well, first things first, I suppose,' Anthea conceded and then added belligerently, 'And don't forget to let him know, while you're at it, that you won't put up with any of the other nonsense either.'

Hayley felt a rush of affection for her friend. 'I don't think I need have any worries in that direction. He already has...a girlfriend.'

Now she knew Marcus Maury a little better she thought the retaliatory kiss he'd given her on the train had been merely a reaction to her challenge to his male pride. What else could it have been, when he already had the vibrantly beautiful Miss Braun in his life?

Anthea cried scornfully, 'Since when's that been any guarantee?'

'Since I met her this afternoon.' Hayley laughed. 'And believe me, even if I wanted to, which I don't, I wouldn't get a look-in.'

'Don't be too sure,' Anthea said darkly.

But Hayley did want to be sure. There was no way she would be able to suffer the furtive gropings... She caught herself up impatiently. Could she really tar every man, including Marcus Maury, with Frank Heaton's squalid brush? The kisses on the train her been at her instigation, forced on him by circumstances. He had kissed her back merely to punish her.

But from the moment she'd stepped through his office door he'd been correctness itself. It was time to regain her sense of perspective. All men were *not* the same, she assured herself desperately. Look at Martin Lukes, who had found it possible to convey friendly admiration without leers or lunges.

'To change the subject,' Hayley said determinedly, 'I'm starving.' She groaned, putting her hand to the aching void that was her stomach. 'Is this really all we have in the larder?'

Anthea stood up with a laugh and ladled beans over two pieces of overdone toast, handing the plate to Hayley.

'No. But it will have to do for tonight. Now you're working I suppose I'll have to take my turn at cooking, but I warn you, I'm no galloping gourmet, and you'll just have to put up with my efforts.'

Hayley groaned. 'If this burnt offering you call toast is any sample of what I can expect, perhaps I'd be better off eating out when it's your turn at the cooker.'

'You may be right. But anyway, we'll certainly be eating out on Saturday.' Anthea grinned widely. 'My day hasn't exactly been without its excitements either. What do you think I managed to get?'

'I don't know.' Hayley eyed her beans without enthusiasm. They were cold and already beginning to congeal unappetisingly. 'Surprise me.'

'Two tickets for the première of Felicity Braun's new film. If you grovel enough I might condescend to take you and stand you a meal later, to celebrate both pieces of good luck.'

Looking at Anthea's glowing face, Hayley tried to feel some excitement. Perhaps it was tiredness, but she felt, perversely, that she'd get more pleasure out of staying at home to wash her hair.

CHAPTER THREE

MARCUS MAURY was already in the office when Hayley arrived next morning, punctually at eight-thirty.

She'd woken with an inexplicable glow...a desire to leap out of bed to start the day. For a moment, still not quite fully conscious, she had been at a loss to explain the phenomenon. It was a long time since she had felt such enthusiasm for work. And then she remembered. It wouldn't be Mr Heaton Senior awaiting her arrival, with Junior lurking in the corridors, but Marcus Maury.

He looked up as she entered his office, to give her an approving nod. 'Glad to see you're punctual, Miss Morgan.'

Hayley fought down the flush which crept beneath her pale creamy skin.

She said, coolly efficient, 'I've brought up the mail. Do you want me to do that first?'

'If you would. Bring it in when you're ready. I'll sort through, but won't be dictating today, unless it's something important. The priority is the minutes of yesterday's meeting. I'd like you to finish them some time today.'

He seemed a little detached, his head lowered again over his diary. Hayley found herself wishing he'd look up and afford her another glance from those blue, blue eyes. But perhaps best not.

Each encounter brought a fresh reminder of his good looks. As always, he was immaculately dressed, this morning in a blue-grey suit and pale blue shirt which enhanced his slight tan and gave him a healthy, virile look that had her trembling inside.

'I should manage it,' she said, determinedly dragging her mind back from forbidden paths, and then wondered why she wanted so much to impress him. She couldn't really understand why it meant so much to her. It wasn't just that she needed the job. 'I was about halfway through yesterday.'

'Good girl.' The sun came out in a blinding flash as he glanced up and smiled, a real smile that deepened the blue of his eyes. Hayley's liberated soul hated the small condescension, but the rest of her couldn't help basking in the brief warmth.

The glow lasted until disaster struck.

Sitting in front of the computer half an hour later, she simply couldn't believe her eyes. The work she'd so carefully saved before leaving yesterday was nowhere to be seen. She'd listed the file in her log under 'Minutes 1', but there was no trace of that file anywhere that it might have been. And though she searched for another hour, she had eventually to give up and accept that, somehow, goodness knew how, she'd lost it.

With the stress he placed on efficiency, the prospect of having to confess the loss to Marcus Maury loomed dauntingly, but she would have to tell him, and it would be better to do so sooner rather than later, because she was going to have to retype the lost work all over again from scratch, which meant there was no chance she would finish the whole thing today.

She got up, with a reluctant sigh, and crossed to his door. He was on the telephone. She couldn't hear what he was saying, but from the softened tone of his voice she guessed he wasn't speaking to a colleague. Probably Felicity Braun, she thought, with a little spurt of irritation.

Her watch said nearly ten-thirty, the time of the official tea-break. Perhaps she should have a cup first, before bearding the lion in his den with the bad news. It might steady her nerves a little too.

The tea room was rather fuller than it had been yesterday afternoon, and Hayley was half tempted to go back to her office. She was in no mood this morning for curious appraisals and whispered remarks.

But the little blonde was there, and Hayley was forced to acknowledge her cheery wave. She got into the small queue at the counter and was less than pleased when the blonde got up to join her.

'I could do with another cup of tea,' the girl said brightly. 'Slaving over a hot computer is thirsty work.'

'Yes.' Hayley's response was unenthusiastic.

'Especially when things go wrong, hey?' She pulled a wry face. 'A whole lot of effort gone up the spout.'

Hayley's attention was caught. 'You've lost something on your computer?'

'Yes, everybody has.' She nodded at Hayley. 'Except you, possibly. I don't suppose you had time to do very much in the way of work on your first day.'

'I did, as a matter of fact. Half the minutes of a very long meeting. And Mr Maury wanted them finished today.'

'Phew!' The girl blew out her cheeks sympathetically. 'You poor thing!'

'Yes,' Hayley agreed glumly. 'How did it happen? Do you know?'

'Not exactly. But we've got a good idea.' She nodded towards the mousy girl with whom she'd been sitting yesterday. 'Theresa's still fairly new here. She's still not sure what she's doing on the computer, and about fourish yesterday afternoon she tried to move a file from one of her own discs into the main computer memory. Nobody, including herself, knows what she did exactly, but it blanked out everybody's screen, losing everything that hadn't already been saved. We all lost something.'

'But I was sure I had saved my work,' Hayley said vexedly. 'I pressed all the right buttons before it vanished.'

The blonde shrugged sympathetically. 'You probably timed it a split second too late to escape from Theresa's blundering efforts.'

Hayley groaned. 'And there's nothing anyone can do?'

'Not that I know of.' Her brow wrinkled in thought. 'Sometimes things get saved on the universal memory, and can be dug up, but I don't know how to get into it. If I did, I'd dig up my own stuff.'

Hayley let out a sigh. Well, at least she wasn't the only one with problems. And it was a relief to know her loss wasn't the result of her own folly. Though how far that would go in saving her from Marcus Maury's annoyance it was difficult to say.

Hayley took him back a black coffee. When he heard what had happened, he'd probably need it. He was off the telephone and hunched over a pile of paperwork on his desk. He looked up with the hint of a smile as she handed him his coffee.

'Thanks.' He took the cup and saucer and made space for it on his littered desk. 'How's it going?'

Hayley had intended waiting until she'd taken a last look through the computer files before saying anything about the lost manuscript, but decided he would be furious, once he did know, that the news had been delayed.

'I'm afraid there's a bit of a problem.'

Briefly, without laying too much emphasis on the inept Theresa's part in the situation, she explained what had happened.

He didn't actually swear aloud, but she saw the movement of his lips. For a moment he closed his eyes as though he couldn't bear to look at her, then he straightened up and asked crisply, 'What's the likelihood of the thing being completed today?'

She shrugged regretfully. 'None at all.'

His jaw tightened irritably.

Hayley noticed it with resentment. It wasn't her fault this had happened. He couldn't really expect her to complete the work by magic, but the failure seemed to hang over her like a cloud.

'I could work through until it was finished, I suppose,' she said doubtfully. 'But I don't know when that would be.'

He looked more angry than pleased at her suggestion.

'That won't be necessary. There's too much day-to-day work to be done here for you to take time off in lieu of overtime.'

'Oh, but I shouldn't automatically want time off. In my other job it was often necessary for me to work overtime. It became part of the job.'

She didn't add that it had been to the exclusion of practically everything else, including her social life. That was partly why it had hurt so much when she found that loyalty hadn't worked both ways.

He nodded coldly. 'I'm sure. But here I'd like you to manage things a little more efficiently, so as to make overtime unnecessary. That way you'll stay bright and alert, with less risk of mistakes, and we'll both be happy.'

His disapproving tone cut Hayley to the quick. His implication was all too obvious. He hadn't completely absolved her from fault with regard to the missing report. She fumed inwardly. She hadn't expected him to be pleased about the situation, but she had hoped he would be fair.

'The delay will mean rearranging some meetings.' He sighed impatiently. 'Remind me in the morning to go through my diary.'

He stood up and began pushing his paperwork back into his briefcase. The grim lines of his face had deepened, making him look older and unexpectedly weary.

Hayley's annoyance faded a little. If he pushed her hard, he pushed himself ever harder.

'Just do what you can,' he said, less brusquely. 'I'll be out for the rest of the day, so you won't have me to worry about.'

He was shrugging into his coat, the day having turned rather chilly, and Hayley found her mind wandering again to the broad, masculine strength of his shoulders and the lithe movements of his body. She gave herself a mental shake as he went on, 'Put the phone calls through to Reception, and Vicki will take the messages.'

Hayley was relieved to see the ghost of a smile on his fascinating lips. To her further surprise, he touched her chin with a finger, holding her to his gaze for a second or two.

'Not such an ogre after all, hey?'

If he expected an answer to that, she couldn't give him one. She was too busy wondering if he had the power to read her mind.

The shock from his touch ran right through her body, and it seemed impossible to unlock her gaze from his. If one finger could do so much, what would it be like...?

With a near superhuman effort she tore her eyes away from his, shaken by the confusion of her feelings . . . half pleasure . . . half resentment at the ease of the charm he used with such devastating effect . . . when it suited him. But at least this time she hadn't recoiled.

After he'd gone Hayley found it difficult to settle to work. She sat for some time with her elbows on her desk and her chin resting in her hands, trying to decide what made Marcus Maury tick, and why, in his presence, she found herself ticking furiously.

Eventually she sat before the computer and opened it up to begin yet another search. Desultorily she went through the routine to bring up the various lists of files, and then suddenly a strange list popped up on to the screen, arranged alphabetically and seemingly endless. Somehow she must have found entry into the universal memory. Quickly she scanned through to M, and there it was! 'Minutes 1'!

She simply couldn't believe her eyes.

Now all she had to do was bring it up into her own system. She did it eventually with the help of her manual, and felt a glow of satisfaction. 'Minutes 1' was back in place, ready for her to take up where she'd left off.

She still couldn't understand what had happened, but wasn't stupid enough to look a gift-horse in the mouth.

Cheered by her unexpected luck, Hayley got down to the business of finishing the minutes. She didn't put the phone through to Reception. After all, Marcus Maury had suggested it only because he'd thought she would have more to do than she now had.

Besides, answering the phone would break the monotony of too much typing, and put her in touch with the people she would be dealing with from now on as the managing director's secretary.

There weren't that many calls of interest, however, until about four-thirty, when Felicity Braun rang, asking to be put through to Marcus Maury right away.

'I'm sorry, Mr Maury is not available at the moment.'

An impatient sigh sounded down the line. 'For pity's sake, don't play the dragon at the gate now. If Marcus is in a meeting or something, just drag him out. I wish to speak to him urgently.'

Hayley tried to keep the frost from her voice. 'Mr Maury isn't in a meeting, Miss Braun. He's out of the office.'

'That tells me a lot,' the actress said snappily. 'Out of the office where?'

'I'm afraid I don't know.' Hayley bit her lip, wishing he'd told her, or that she'd had the sense to ask him. 'He didn't say.'

'New at this game, are you?' Felicity asked disparagingly. 'Well, if this is your best performance, I don't think you're going to last long.'

If you have anything to do with it I probably won't, Hayley retorted silently, but aloud she said, 'I'm sorry, Miss Braun. I'll tell Mr Maury you called.'

'Yes. Do that! If I don't tell him first.' The phone was slammed down with a resounding clatter that rang in Hayley's head for some time afterwards.

He came in about half an hour later, with a frown on his face that seemed to spell trouble for someone.

'Get me a cup of coffee, will you?' he commanded, without preamble.

The serving hatch in the staff-room was closed, but, in answer to Hayley's knock, it opened and a disgruntled face appeared in the aperture.

'You're too late. Everything's cold and I'm not making any fresh.'

'It's not for me,' Hayley explained hastily. 'Mr Maury wants a coffee. Black, no sugar.'

'I know how he likes it. I've been here long enough.'

The disdainful sniff left Hayley in no doubt that the lady felt that her length of service gave her the edge over any new upstart.

He was sitting behind his desk when she eventually returned with the steaming cup, studying the file containing the completed minutes, a puzzled expression in place of the earlier grimness.

'You finished all this today?' he queried as she set the cup on the heat-resistant pad on his highly polished desk. 'What are you, Miss Morgan? Some kind of superwoman?'

'Unfortunately not.' Hayley would have liked to claim the title, but couldn't. 'I finished it only because the universal memory magically appeared on my screen. Don't ask me how.'

He grunted shortly. 'Then I won't. But are you sure it wasn't there all the time?'

'I'm sure it wasn't. I searched for it for over an hour this morning. Later I found it somewhere quite different.'

He studied her face silently, the blue eyes deliberately unreadable, until her colour began to rise with discomfort. Then he said musingly, 'In my book, honesty ranks more than equal to capability. Some, probably most, might have lied by omission and just taken the credit.'

Hayley let out the breath she hadn't known she'd been holding.

'Too risky,' she said. 'You might have expected me to repeat such a feat at some time in the future, and then what a fool I'd have looked.'

His brows rose. 'Sound reasoning, Miss Morgan.' His mouth quirked sardonically at one corner. 'Clear logic is almost as much an asset as a beautiful face.'

Chauvinistic comment! she thought in silent annoyance, but the underlying implication had her pulse jumping erratically, and when she couldn't bear to go on looking into those disquieting blue depths any longer she turned away.

Glancing down at her notebook, she said a little unevenly, 'By the way, Miss Braun phoned.'

'I know.' The tone of his voice had changed, and she looked up quickly. The grimness was back. 'I called her earlier and she told me you were rather less than helpful.'

Hayley bit her lip. Her moment as paragon hadn't lasted long! She could just imagine the comments made by Felicity Braun, with the incident blown up out of all proportion. 'It wasn't intentional.'

He grimaced. 'Why didn't you put the phone through to Vicki in Reception as I told you?'

'There didn't seem any point, when I could manage myself.'

Brusquely he said, 'There was a point. Vicki was informed of my movements; you weren't. Next time, follow instructions. It will save us all a lot of trouble.'

Hayley bit her lip. 'I'm sorry.' She seemed always to be apologising for something, she thought a little resentfully.

He gave a deep sigh and reached for his coffee. To her surprise, the look he gave her over the rim of his cup held a glint of humour.

'Swings and roundabouts, Miss Morgan,' he said. 'Life's full of them.'

Which was certainly true of the rest of the week. So many swings and roundabouts that she was positively giddy. In the past she'd always managed to round the week off tidily, with everything that needed to be done completed by Friday. But when Friday came, the in-tray was still very much in.

Marcus Maury had been out for the whole day, which was a blessing, since it allowed her to bash on unhindered. This time she did put her telephone through to the receptionist, with a silent blessing for the obliging Vicki.

The girl came up towards the end of the afternoon with a list of messages.

'Still in the thick of things, I see.' She grinned. 'Rather you than me. And if you think you'll be really late leaving, don't forget to let the porter know, because of the security system.'

Hayley nodded, without ceasing the flight of her fingers over the computer keys. 'Thanks a lot, Vicki. Have a good weekend.'

'Oh, I will. Don't worry.' She was a pretty girl, with a carefree smile. 'Have you got anything special on?'

'Not really,' Hayley said absently, and then, as she recalled, 'Oh, my flatmate has two tickets for the première of Felicity Braun's new film tomorrow night. I might go.'

Vicki snorted. 'Don't you see enough of her around the office?'

Hayley grimaced. 'That's a point.'

The actress had been buzzing in and out the whole week, and Hayley wondered how she could spare the time. Probably 'resting' in between films, she decided a little cattily. And making the most of the opportunity to keep Marcus Maury's interest at fever pitch. Though why that should bother Hayley she didn't know, and at the moment she was too busy even to hunt for reasons.

Remembering Marcus's ban on overtime, she felt momentarily guilty. But he wasn't here to see, and she did have the weekend ahead to get over it.

Eventually the last letter was typed and placed in the folder for his signature. She took it through into his office.

The room smelled faintly of his aftershave, which sent a strange little tingle up Hayley's spine, making her shiver. She looked up at the portrait of him, which hung majestically behind his desk. He was wearing a dark, formal suit and looked very forbidding. And there was that little shiver again. What was it about this man that lured her into daydreaming? Hadn't she reason enough to avoid such foolishness like the plague?

The building was quiet now and she had time to notice how late it was. She hadn't meant to stay so long.

What was it Vicki had said about the security system and the porter? She hadn't really been listening. She soon found out when she tried to open her office door. It was shut fast, and unresponsive to all her efforts to open it. Then she noticed the little code panel alongside, and groaned. A combination lock, which would only open the door to the right sequence. Now what was she going to do?

A bubble of panic threatened to rise, but she pushed it down determinedly. Perhaps there was still somebody in the building . . . the porter in the lobby, or someone else working late. She picked up the telephone and clicked the rest up and down a few times, hoping someone might see or hear something on the switchboard, but nothing happened. She slammed it down hard in frustration.

She thought about ringing Anthea, but her friend would probably be at the hairdresser's by now. She had an evening appointment and had gone straight from her office, which was partly why Hayley had decided to work on. In any case, even if she could get hold of her, not knowing the code, Anthea wouldn't be any real help in getting her out of the building.

The police could probably help, but she was reluctant to involve them in her foolish situation. Marcus Maury was going to be annoyed enough about her deliberately disobeying yet another of his instructions, without her dragging the authorities into it.

And he was right. Every time she deliberately went against him, she found herself in trouble.

Which was why she held out so long before deciding to telephone him.

In the end, of course, she had to accept that it was the only solution. She found his home number in his diary and dialled, sighing with frustration when she got his answering machine. Having worked herself up to this, her nerve was shaken by the disappointment. She was tempted just to replace the receiver, but steeled herself to leave a message, trying not to speculate on his feelings when he heard it.

Now there really was nothing to do but wait until he either came to let her out or telephoned her.

But after half an hour had passed she began to wonder whether he might not be away for the weekend, and felt a tremor that could easily become a quake. Firmly she pulled herself together.

Using the logic he'd admired, she examined her situation. The very worst that could happen was that she would be here for the weekend, until the system was unlocked on Monday morning. The thought was unnerving, to say the least, but she thrust down the desire to panic. That wouldn't get her anywhere. And anyway, it was unlikely to come to that. A more likely occurrence was that the cleaners would arrive at some time before then. Probably on Saturday morning.

To take her mind off the situation, she worked on the backlog of filing and, with that done, she went into Marcus Maury's office to start on his out-tray. She sat at his desk, in his chair, realising with surprise that, even without his presence, it was a comfort.

After a little while she sat back with a tired sigh and closed her eyes, letting her mind wander. The first time she'd seen him, on the train, he'd been sitting like this, with his eyes closed. The familiar grim expression had been absent then, and his face, she remembered with a little spurt of excitement, had been relaxed and very handsome. She squirmed with renewed embarrassment. How had she ever have had the nerve to do what she'd done?

But, strangely, she didn't now regret the incident. Her only regret was that she hadn't made the kiss a real one . . . allowed herself to feel it. An opportunity missed that would never come again.

And he hadn't mentioned it again. She'd wanted him to forget, and now it seemed that he had. The incident was memorable to her, but not necessarily so to him. Perhaps strange women kissed him all the time. The thought had been meant as a joke, but stirred an irrational feeling of annoyance.

For heaven's sake, she remonstrated with herself. He belongs to Felicity Braun, and you, my girl, know well enough where infatuation during working hours can lead. But then she hadn't been the one who'd been infatuated. And she wasn't now. Not if she could do anything about it.

She must have dozed eventually, because she came to with a little start, her heart pounding as she tried to orientate herself. She was somewhere in a darkened room, and there was a noise that threatened danger. There was a faint light from somewhere, and suddenly, silhouetted in the doorway, a figure loomed. She screamed, jumping to her feet in fright.

A startled male voice said, 'What the hell...?'

A light snapped on, and Marcus Maury stood looking at her in amazement.

'Miss Morgan! What on earth...?'

As fright gave way to relief she rushed towards him, stumbling over the rug on the polished floor. He caught her up before she fell and held her steady against him.

Involuntarily, her arms went around his neck and she clung to him, her breath coming in little gasps. 'Oh! Thank God! I thought I'd never get out.'

Only now, when rescue finally had come, did she let herself feel the full dread of her situation, and she began to shake uncontrollably.

He gathered her close, his hand moving soothingly against her back. She felt the strength of him, the hard outline of his body against hers, the firm but gentle clasp of his arms about her, and her fright began to subside.

Suddenly self-conscious, she began gently to disentangle herself from him.

'For heaven's sake,' he said, as she continued to tremble, 'calm down and tell me what you're doing here.'

Reluctantly she moved away, looking up into his face rather sheepishly before trying to explain. 'I got locked in. I stayed to finish the last of the letters and then found I couldn't get out.'

He made a sharp sound of annoyance. 'I seem to remember making my opinions on that point quite clear to you.'

Hayley felt a ridiculous urge to hang her head, but with an effort she kept her gaze steady.

'I know. But I had some time to spare and I wanted to clear the decks ready for Monday.'

She saw the ice-blue glint of anger in his eyes, and her own eyes widened on his in anticipation of what she knew would come.

'Has it always been impossible for you to do as you're told?' he gritted.

Hayley answered with attack. 'Isn't your secretary ever allowed to be a little spontaneous?'

He said harshly, 'Within the rules—occasionally. But if she's doing her job competently, it shouldn't be——'

'Don't talk to me about competence,' Hayley spat back at him. 'I don't suppose it occurred to you to tell me about the security system. If you had, this wouldn't have happened.'

'This wouldn't have happened anyway, if you knew how to obey orders.'

He shook her forcefully until her teeth rattled, and then, without warning, pulled her into his arms, crushing her lips beneath his with punishing force, his hold like steel about her slender form.

Taken off guard, Hayley tried to resist, but it was futile. This was no Frank Heaton, weak and flabby, but a man made out of rock, against whom it was impossible to fight. If he wanted, he could ... She felt the clutch of an old fear.

A frightened whimper sounded in her throat, and almost immediately his head lifted a little to release her lips.

'Please,' she whispered hoarsely. 'Let me go.'

His breathing was rapid, his face faintly flushed, and in the blue eyes was no hint of remorse, only anger.

'What is it about you, girl, that drives me ...?' With a furious sound, he put her from him.

Hayley's fear had been replaced by a matching anger. 'So now it's my fault that you act like a beast,' she ranted. 'Why is it that men, the so-called stronger sex, always have to pin the blame elsewhere? If it's not short skirts and tight sweaters that tip men over the edge, it's simple errors of judgement that any reasonable person would understand.'

'I don't know what skirts and sweaters have to do with it, and your error wasn't reasonable,' he retaliated, his own eyes blazing, his fingers gripping her arms so tightly that it hurt. 'It was sheer bloody-minded cussedness. You just can't obey the simplest——'

'Cussedness?' Hayley echoed loudly, her temper beyond control. 'Of course that's how you would see it. You arrogant, unreasonable, pigheaded...' She ran out of breath and adjectives to describe him. 'You wouldn't recognise conscientiousness if it bit you, nor a desire to...'

In the heat of her fury, she caught herself up. What was she trying to tell him? That she been filled by a desire to what? To impress him, to please him? Why, when he was everything she despised?

And why was she trembling, her heart burning, like her face, with the confusion of her emotions?

And why was she letting him take her again into his arms—gently this time, pressing her head to his chest, speaking her name on a despairing note? 'Hayley. You little fool. What am I going to do with you?'

Hayley, with her face muffled against his shirt, could give him no answer. She was struggling with a dam that seemed about to burst. All the tension and humiliation of the past months seemed to be gathering in a great lump in her chest, pressing behind her eyes, until she felt something, somewhere had to give...

But not now. Not with him.

She pulled herself away from him, delving shakily into her pocket for a handkerchief and finding none.

He took an immaculately folded square from his top pocket and handed it to her.

'Here. Use this.'

She took it and blew her nose noisily, turning away a little with her eyes lowered. The urge to cry began to fade. Eventually, she dared to look up.

He was in control again—detached, cool, as he strode away from her towards his desk, riffling through the papers, giving her time to pull herself together.

Hayley watched him, the trim, muscular lines of his body, the confident movements of his lean hands, and felt a tremor of response to that strong animal magnetism, so potent, and seemingly so natural.

He strode back towards her, his blue eyes showing impatience now.

'Am I never going to get through to you that I emphatically mean what I say? Unless you're prepared to listen, we're never going to get along.'

Hayley gripped her lower lip between her teeth for a second and then said quietly, 'Perhaps you'd like me to give you my resignation.'

He made a sharp sound. 'Oh, that would be wonderful. Then what would I do? Waste more time looking around for someone else to take your place?'

Hayley felt the frustration of the double bind. He didn't want *her*; it was obvious by the irritation showing clearly on his face. He would be keeping her on only to suit his own purposes.

'Wouldn't that be better than putting up with someone who just can't seem to get it right?'

For a second he stared down at her. 'You could get it right, if you wanted.'

To her dismay she found herself saying, 'I do want to. And I try so hard...'

Their eyes met, hers clouded with uncertainty, his probing deeply, searching for something that seemed to elude him.

Then he swore softly under his breath.

'It's time you went home. You've had a nerve-racking experience.' His expression was unreadable now. 'Perhaps this isn't the time or place for the riot act.'

Hayley sniffed, beginning to feel more like herself. 'Oh, go on! Read the riot act, damn you. You will anyway, sooner or later. We might just as well get it over with.'

He laughed, and she looked up with a reluctant smile, her cheeks flushed, her velvet-brown eyes still a little hazy from repressed tears.

He groaned, as though in torment, and then suddenly he was kissing her again, his mouth warm and arousing on hers. His long fingers slipped into the knot of her hair, loosening it so that his hand cupped the sensitive nape of her neck.

In Hayley there was no resistance now...no fear. She shuddered as a strange thrill shot up her spine, and involuntarily she moulded herself against him, her own arms slipping about his waist, her hands moving upwards against the hard muscle of his back as the kiss deepened, drawing her ever deeper into a whirlpool of emotions too complex to distinguish.

Her mind battled against this surrender. Why was she letting him do this? Hadn't she vowed to keep her distance? She'd have no one but herself to blame if she let this go too far.

She moaned and made a feeble effort to pull away, but he drew her back again, his hold tightening, his lips becoming firm and demanding, exciting her to further spasms of delight.

He took his hand from her neck and wrapped his arms about her until he felt her taut body arch against him. Then his hands began to caress her waist, her back, her ribcage, long fingers brushing lightly against the sides of her breasts, never touching, but filling her with the heat of anticipation.

His hands moved down her spine, and caressed the gentle swell of her buttocks, making her aware of the strength of his arousal. A little gasp was forced from her, and for a moment he hesitated.

Hayley felt the slackening of his hold with a sense of inexplicable despair. He had brought her to the brink of something so unlike anything she had ever experienced. It would be cruel now to draw her back.

Involuntarily she gripped him and then relaxed her hold as he began gently to disentangle himself from her.

Her face was already flooding with colour as he moved back to look down at her.

'Come on.' He turned her gently towards the door. 'Let's get out of here. I'll take you home.'

Reality came rushing back, and with it a surge of self-disgust. At the serious test, all her good intentions had gone winging out of the window. Not only had she failed to defend herself against his advances, she had actually encouraged them, willed him to go on, despaired when he had been the one to draw away.

There was no way she could travel home with him in the intimate confines of his car. She hardly knew how she was ever going to face him again at the office.

She said tightly, 'There's no need for you to take me home. The buses are quite frequent. I shouldn't have to wait long.'

'You won't have to wait at all,' he said imperiously. 'I intend to deliver you safely to your doorstep.' And, as she opened her mouth to protest, he raised his hand. 'Don't argue. It's pointless.'

She'd been right to feel nervous about travelling in the car with him. His presence filled the luxurious interior, and her enforced nearness to him shortened her breath. It was becoming less and less easy to understand why their first meeting had caused so little disturbance to her emotions.

It was a relief when they turned finally into the street of terraced houses where Anthea had her flat.

'This will be fine,' she said, indicating a gap at the kerb. 'You didn't really have to go to the trouble of bringing me home, but thanks anyway.'

'No trouble.' He was gazing curiously out of the window. 'Is this your place?'

'Not exactly. The flat belongs to a friend. We share it.'

He nodded. 'I see. Is your friend at home?'

'Probably. Unless she's still at the hairdresser's.'

He seemed to relax. 'Will you be all right until she returns?'

Oppressed now by self-consciousness, Hayley couldn't wait to get out of the car. 'Don't worry. I'll be fine.'

'Good.' He seemed suddenly detached and said, almost sharply, 'Remind me on Monday to give you the combinations for the security system.'

Safely in the flat, she made herself a cup of tea, and then left it to go cold as her mind went over the events of the evening. She had broken all her own rules, and it would be hard, in view of her undeniable response to him, even to attempt to defend her principles against him in the future. Perhaps she should give in her notice after all. It might be the only way to save her pride. She would decide on Monday, when she'd faced the ordeal of meeting him again.

She decided to say nothing to Anthea about the affair, and then occupied ten minutes trying to understand her reluctance to discuss anything to do with Marcus Maury with her friend. In the past, growing up together in their small home town, nothing had been secret.

Was it a sign of maturity not to want to be an open book, she asked herself pensively, or was she simply afraid there would be questions Anthea might ask to which Hayley couldn't or wouldn't find the answers? She had a strong suspicion it was the latter.

CHAPTER FOUR

HAYLEY was glad, for Anthea's sake, that she hadn't had to miss the première. Her friend's excitement was contagious, and in the end Hayley found herself looking forward to the event and the meal afterwards.

The fiasco of the night before had been pushed firmly from her mind. She excused them both by deciding that what had happened had been an overcharged response to the tension of the moment and that Marcus Maury would be as anxious to forget it as she was.

What had depressed her last night now seemed to have a positive side. For his own reasons, he was as reluctant to dispense with her services as she was to give up the benefits of a good salary and a job which would enhance her experience when looking for a new job. If she could just hang on to that realisation, her battered pride might manage to survive.

She tried not to remember what it had been like to be in his arms. Each time the disturbing memories forced their way into her consciousness she turned her mind deliberately to other things.

It helped that Anthea talked of nothing else but the première, although, in turn, that reminded Hayley of Felicity Braun's involvement with Marcus, and for some reason she didn't want to think about that either.

She did, in wayward moments, wonder what Felicity would think if she knew Hayley had been in Marcus's arms the night before. Not that she revelled in the thought. It added nothing to her opinion of his character. On the contrary, it only confirmed her suspicion that all men were untrustworthy to one degree or another.

The film was good, and Felicity Braun, as always, gave a faultless performance. Surprisingly, though, the fact that Hayley now knew the actress personally seemed to spoil things, though in quite what way she couldn't say.

'Wasn't she great?' Anthea enthused as they walked out together into the foyer at the end of the evening. 'What wouldn't I give to look just like her?' She pushed dissatisfied hands through her bright yellow hair which always seemed to stand on end no matter how carefully she brushed it. 'A change of colour would be easy enough, and I might even manage the hairstyle ... given a good hairdresser.'

'Given a wizard of a hairdresser, you still couldn't beat that mop into submission,' Hayley retorted, feeling strangely annoyed. 'Besides, I like you just the way you are. Human.'

'Bit of a back-handed compliment, that,' Anthea responded, with a despairing shrug of her shoulders. 'I wouldn't mind, but it's the only kind I seem to get these days.'

She gripped Hayley's arm. 'Oh, look! There's Felicity Braun. She's signing autographs. I've just got to get one.'

Hayley groaned. 'Oh, for heaven's sake, Anthea. Autographs are for adolescents. Besides, it could take hours, and I'm starving. If you hang about we'll never get a taxi to the restaurant.'

'Then we'll walk,' Anthea said determinedly, digging for a pen in her voluminous bag. 'You're so stuffy these days,' she accused, before issuing the command, 'Wait there!'

Hayley grabbed her arm. 'Look! I'll ...'

She ground to a halt as Anthea's expectant gaze turned on her. She'd been about to say she would get an autograph from Felicity next time she saw her in the office, but of course she couldn't. Anthea would be furious if she knew Hayley had kept that big a secret from her.

'Oh, go on!' she said irritably. 'I'll wait.'

Under the press of enthusiastic autograph hunters, Hayley was forced to retreat close to the wall of the foyer. She occupied some minutes studying the stills of the film. She had reluctantly to admit that Felicity Braun looked stunning in her period costumes. A creature, almost, from another world.

Feeling suddenly wretched, she wondered how Marcus Maury even found time to notice the existence of other women, with a beauty like Felicity to fill his love-life. But her own personal experience had shown her he managed it.

Her soft mouth drew into a hard line. Weren't most men the same? Opportunists! Ready and willing to take advantage of any situation which might offer a few cheap thrills and a boost to their massive egos.

She knew she was generalising a little freely, but in her present frame of mind she didn't feel at all like being fair.

Even Marcus Maury, hardly an example of the average man, hadn't been above making the most of an opportunity. But honesty forbade her to criticise him too forcefully when, admittedly in the grip of fright and relief, she'd practically thrown herself into his arms. But that had only been the first time. The second time, he had been the one to...

The memory of his kisses, the thrilling strangeness of his hands caressing her body, arousing undreamt-of sensations, came back with disturbing clarity, making her groan. A pain, as sharp as any with a physical cause, shot through her chest. She closed her eyes and clutched her hand to her breast, holding her breath until the spasm passed.

'Well, hello, Miss Morgan!'

The deep, pleasant voice spoke almost in Hayley's ear, making her jump. Her eyes flew open in startled surprise and she let out her pent-up breath in a little gasp.

Marcus Maury's blue eyes beheld her with amusement.

'Are you sure this is the right place for meditation?'

She coloured. 'I was . . . resting my eyes.'

His mouth curved in a smile that deepened the lines in his cheeks. 'You should have worn your spectacles,' he observed kindly. 'Or do you wear them only to hide those lovely eyes? Which, by the way, speak more clearly than words.'

He touched her cheek, tracing the delicate bones with a light finger. 'To think you could look like this all the time. Why don't you?'

'Don't do that!' she commanded sharply, refusing to answer the taunt.

She flinched away, her colour deepening. How much of her reactions to him did he understand? And did he think that just because she'd let him kiss her it gave him *carte blanche* to behave as he wished, even in public?

A little desperately, she looked across to the crowd around Felicity Braun, groaning silently as she saw Anthea's yellow hair bobbing about, obviously still some way from her goal.

'Are you waiting for someone?'

She said tightly, 'Yes. A friend.' She nodded towards the crowd. She wished she could say it was a man, but he'd find out the truth soon enough. 'She's waiting for an autograph.'

He smiled. 'The flatmate who so admires Miss Braun?'

She nodded, thinking there wasn't much he didn't notice or remember. Which made it all the more important to keep a guard on her tongue and her apparently give-away eyes.

How could he be so casual, as though last night had never happened? But then, of course, it hadn't been important to him.

'I have a feeling you may have to wait a little longer.' He was appraising her openly, with every evidence of enjoyment.

'Yes, I think I might,' she muttered in vexation, wishing, without any real hope of it happening, that he'd go away.

Moving restlessly under his gaze, Hayley wished that she'd thought this evening's outing through a little more carefully. If she had, she would have realised Marcus Maury was bound to be here. Then, instead of wearing her midnight-blue dress, which fitted her curves like a second skin, and *diamanté* slides in her thick dark hair, set free now to curl luxuriantly, she definitely *would* have worn her glasses *and* her chignon.

She had to admit *he* looked simply devastating in a formal dress-suit and sparkling white shirt. Her gaze seemed magnetised to the sternly handsome face, in which his eyes glinted coolly.

To escape her embarrassment, she turned her head to scan the room. Mercifully, the crowds seemed to be melting away, and Anthea's bright head was bobbing in her direction.

'Well, it looks as though my friend's mission is accomplished,' she said thankfully, beginning to move away. 'See you on Monday morning.'

To her surprise, he reached out and caught her arm, pulling her back towards him. 'Do you mind if I see you *now* for a few seconds longer?'

She raised her eyes to his, wondering if she looked as hunted as she felt.

'That business at the office...' he began.

Hayley's heart leapt awkwardly. So he did have some feelings of guilt about that. Oh, my God! Was he going to ask her to keep quiet about it in front of Felicity? She wouldn't be able to bear it if he did.

Anthea had almost reached them, her face aglow. She halted as she realised her friend was talking to a man. She stood politely at a distance, waiting for them to finish. Not that either was talking at that moment.

Marcus Maury was taking his time in studying Hayley's face, and Hayley was staring back at him, her mouth half open while she found the words to tell him what she thought of him, but before she could collect herself he said, 'I'd intended calling on you tomorrow, to make sure there were no ill effects.'

He was talking about her ordeal, she realised incredulously, not their lovemaking.

'There aren't any,' she said faintly. 'Ill effects, I mean.'

He smiled. 'That's good.'

But something unfathomable still hung in the air between them.

Was he, the great, commanding Marcus Maury, afraid to ask her for what he wanted?

'And as for...the...other,' she said, skirting delicately around the words she couldn't bring herself to say, 'don't worry. I've already forgotten all about it.'

His brows rose the merest fraction. 'Really? How crushing to my ego.' Something tugged at the corner of his mouth, and Hayley had a suspicion that he was actually laughing at her.

'You'll survive,' she said grimly. 'And perhaps, in future, you should indulge your romantic inclinations only where they're welcome.'

He frowned. 'I could have sworn that's precisely what I was doing. Could I really have been so mistaken?'

Hayley drew in a sharp breath. 'You've got to be the most arrogant...conceited...' She fumed, silently mouthing adjectives she didn't dare to utter.

He moved closer, and she felt his warm breath fanning her forehead. 'Is it conceit to say honestly what you feel?' he challenged, barely audibly. 'You should try it some time, Hayley. Being honest, I mean.'

Hayley blinked at the familiar use of her name, and, despite her anger, it sent a shiver of pleasure up her receptive spine.

'Then perhaps we might get somewhere.'

She licked dry lips. 'And where is it that you want to get, Mr Maury? With me, I mean. Isn't one string to your bow enough?'

His eyes narrowed on hers in silence for some seconds, the cool probing of his gaze drawing her nerves so taut that she felt she'd scream.

Then he said, 'Perhaps. But it would need to be the right string to strike the desired chord.'

While Hayley was still trying to digest this, and find a reply, an excited voice sounded in her ear.

'Oh, my gosh! It *is* you!' They both turned as Anthea's breathless voice broke between them. 'Sorry to interrupt, but I simply can't believe it.' She turned her round, incredulous eyes on Marcus Maury. 'You really are Felicity Braun's——'

Hayley saw the furious darkening of his expression with dismay. There was no way anyone would describe Marcus Maury as anyone's anything, and get away with it.

She cut in quickly. 'Anthea, I think you should meet my—er—boss. Mr Marcus Maury.'

The hesitation must have shown him plainly that she believed that relationship might now be in doubt, and she saw a gleam of something in his eyes that looked like ironic amusement. Well, let him have the satisfaction of his little private joke, she thought tightly. She wasn't that desperate for a job.

'This is *him*?' Anthea repeated in amazement. 'Why, you sly puss, Hayley. You didn't tell me he was also——'

Hayley trod on Anthea's foot hard, quite unmoved by her friend's glare of pained outrage.

It was at that moment Felicity Braun joined them, her hand slipping possessively through Marcus Maury's arm.

'Here I am at last, darling! Did it seem like forever?' Her eyes gleamed coolly as she realised he was in company. 'I might have known you'd manage to find a little diversion. Double helpings too, you greedy thing.'

Ignoring the coy reproach, Marcus Maury said abruptly, 'You've met Miss Morgan already at the office. And although I haven't yet been introduced, this young lady is, I take it, Miss Morgan's friend. Miss—er...?'

'Lewis.' Anthea supplied hastily. 'Thank you so much for your autograph, Miss Braun.' The piece of paper waved in her hand.

'Only too happy,' Felicity said, but she was looking closely at Hayley's flushed face.

'This is *Miss Morgan*?' She eyed Hayley coldly. 'Well! She's certainly been keeping her light well hidden underneath a bushel.'

He gave a grim laugh. 'Yes. There I have to agree.'

Hayley gave a little shudder at the hard gleam in his blue eyes, and groaned silently as he went on, 'In fact we were just discussing her penchant for hiding.'

Hayley muttered something rude beneath her breath.

'We've booked to eat,' she said, trying to sound nonchalant. 'So I'll see you on Monday, Mr Maury.'

He inclined his head. 'Goodnight, Miss Morgan.'

'Goodnight,' she muttered, unable to meet his eyes. 'Goodnight, Miss Braun. Wonderful film.'

'Oh, yes,' Anthea chirped in admiringly. 'We both enjoyed it enormously.'

Felicity ignored them both.

Still looking bemused, Anthea allowed herself to be dragged away. Thankfully Hayley led her outside into the fresh air, where, as luck would have it, a taxi was just drawing into the kerb. Grabbing Anthea's arm, she sprinted forward to beat another couple who'd been waiting.

'Sorry,' she said as she bundled Anthea into the back. 'It's an emergency.'

If she had any more emergencies in the near future, she thought grimly, then she was probably in for a nervous breakdown.

Anthea had booked at an Italian restaurant, and, although she normally loved Italian food, Hayley doubted she would be able to do full justice to her favourite cannelloni tonight.

Anthea was sulking a little. Now the excitement had worn off, she was hurt by what she called Hayley's deviousness.

'Why didn't you tell me who he was?' she complained, while trying to juggle with meatballs and trailing spaghetti.

'I didn't think it was important,' Hayley hedged, still reluctant to discuss Marcus Maury with Anthea. Especially after their disturbing conversation, which had led—goodness knew where. Come Monday, she might not even be his secretary anyway.

'Important?' Anthea was saying explosively. 'You didn't think working for Felicity Braun's latest was important?'

Hayley's frayed temper seemed close to snapping. 'I wish you'd stop saying that. Latest what? Latest besotted admirer? Latest groupie?' Hayley gave a short, hard laugh. 'If you knew Marcus Maury, you would know he's not the type of person to fit happily into either of those descriptions.'

Good grief, what's the matter with me? she thought disbelievingly. I'm actually defending his integrity.

Unrepentant, Anthea grinned. 'Latest lover, I should think. There was definitely something sparking between those two. She was practically gobbling him up with those fascinating green-gold eyes of hers.'

Hayley didn't like the description, although she had to admit it fitted.

'I didn't notice,' she said untruthfully. 'Now do you mind if I forget all about work, and Marcus Maury, and enjoy my meal?'

It would have been nice if she could have done, but, no matter how hard she tried, her mind came back to him. Because of her stupid need to impress him—and that, she now recognised, was what the nonsense of working late had been all about—their relationship had been changed irrevocably.

Last night he had found out how easy it was to get her into his arms. Did he intend to take advantage of that fact, as Frank Heaton undoubtedly would have? she wondered, worrying into the early hours of the morning, when the only partially digested cannelloni lay as heavily on her chest as the foreboding did on her mind.

CHAPTER FIVE

MARCUS was already there when Hayley arrived first thing Monday morning. He'd obviously brought the mail up early, and was sorting it when she walked through into his office.

She'd been reluctant to face him, unsure what his attitude this morning would be, and had had to steel herself to walk calmly into his room.

He lifted his head in response to her wary, 'Good morning.'

'I see you've started the post,' she said crisply. 'Would you like me to finish it?'

To her consternation, his hand came out to grasp hers as she leaned across his desk, his long, lean fingers tensile against her skin.

'Leave it for a moment,' he ordered casually, absently moving his thumb against the soft, sensitive skin of her wrist, filling her with a painful confusion. Did he know how easily he could affect her with his slightest touch? She felt the flow of his vitality and stifled a shudder, pulling her hand from his.

He sat back, perfectly at ease, as his eyes flicked over her in absorbed and silent appraisal.

Hayley squirmed under his scrutiny, longing to tell him to stop, but she didn't want to start a quarrel this early in the morning if she could avoid it. She longed to know what it was that held him entranced.

She wore a straight black skirt and neat blouse and had coiled her hair, but she wasn't wearing her glasses.

His mouth curved sardonically, and at last he said, 'I see you're still wearing the disguise. Now you've been rumbled, I don't quite see the point of keeping it up.'

Hayley flushed. 'It isn't a disguise. It's simply my idea of suitable dress for the office.' She added spiritedly, 'You wouldn't wear a business suit to play tennis, would you?'

He grinned, his teeth gleaming white against his lightly tanned skin.

Hayley's stomach gave its familiar little lurch as her eyes were caught in his ironic gaze.

'Actually my game's squash, not tennis, but point taken.'

He stood up and came around the desk, his eyes on her hair. 'It wouldn't hurt to let that glorious hair free, though, would it?' Unexpectedly, his fingers loosened the knot, allowing the curls their freedom to riot, and she moved back out of his reach with a cry of annoyance.

'The way I wear my hair is my choice. And I happen to like it pinned up.' She held her hand out for the pins he'd removed, and he gave them to her with a sigh.

'Shame!' he said mockingly, as she drew the hair forcibly back from her face and re-coiled it. 'It's so pretty, and actually I'm not averse to a little glamour about the office, provided it comes hand in glove with efficiency.'

Her brown eyes glinted fiery sparks. She said coldly, 'The efficiency I can promise you.'

His brows rose mockingly. 'And the glamour?'

She shrugged. 'Out of place, don't you think? I wouldn't like to be thought provocative.' Old memories resurfaced, making her bitter.

'An admirable sentiment.' His laugh this time was full of amusement. 'I'd be more impressed if I hadn't met a certain Miss Pushy on a train, who showed every sign of being provocative.'

Hayley grimaced. She'd thought it was too good to last. 'Oh, I see! So we're back to that.'

'Yes. You never did reveal the mystery.'

She shook her head. 'Ancient history, Mr Maury. No longer topical.'

'But tantalising. I'd like to know. Why won't you tell me?' His voice was soft, almost seductive, and he moved forward, so close that she was pinned with her back against the desk.

Her heart fluttered uncomfortably. She felt trapped, by the past and its power to invade the present. And by the determination of this man to pierce every one of her defences.

She said tensely, 'Because it's none of your damned business.'

The smile had vanished, to be replaced by a frown. 'I think anything that involves me becomes my business.'

'And I disagree.'

It was difficult not to be intimidated, especially since his face was so close that she could feel the warmth of him and smell the subtle scent of his aftershave, which sent her treacherous heart leaping about like a lamb in spring.

He went on staring into her defiant eyes for seconds that seemed like years, before giving a resigned shrug. 'What's new?'

His hands lifted and she thought for a moment that he was about to seize her shoulders, but they halted midway and fell to his sides.

Walking back around the desk, he sat down heavily, his face withdrawn and unreadable.

Unaccountably she was shaking and, intimidated by his sudden withdrawal, she wondered if, once again, she'd gone too far. 'I can promise Miss Pushy is out of your life forever. And Miss Morgan wants only to do her job as well as circumstances will allow. We can agree on that.'

He gave her a wintry smile. 'Well, I suppose that's something.' He pushed the paperwork across the desk. 'Now you can have the post.'

*   *   *

After that awkward start things could only get better, Hayley promised herself. But in the weeks that followed they went from busy to hectic, and as yet another weekend loomed Hayley's in-tray was still very much 'in'. But, she thought wryly, there was no danger of her making the mistake of working over this weekend.

Mid-afternoon on Friday, Hayley felt as she imagined Atlas must have felt, carrying the world on his shoulders, and decided to put it down for a while, to take a desperately needed break.

She brought a cup of tea and a sticky bun up from the tea-room and was indulging herself, seated at her desk, when her door began to open. She'd been expecting Marcus to come back for the past hour, and had a half-smile pinned to her lips, awaiting the ribald remark she knew would come, when the door opened further and, with some difficulty, a woman manoeuvred a wheelchair into her office.

The stranger had a long, thin face, set with sharp grey eyes which fixed on Hayley's snack with obvious disgust.

'When the cat's away...' she said pointedly, adding frostily, 'And if there's one thing Marcus hates, it's eating in the office.'

Hayley was tempted to say that, far from hating her taking her break in her room, he was only too delighted, as long as it kept the work moving forward, but why should she stoop to argue with this stranger?

'Is there something I can do for you?' she asked as politely as she could manage.

'Not you,' the woman said, with a cool smile. 'There is something, but I'd prefer to discuss it with Marcus.'

With a similarly cool smile Hayley answered, 'I'm afraid he isn't here at the moment.'

'That's pretty obvious.' The grey eyes were looking pointedly at the bun again. 'But don't worry about me.' She waved her hand airily. 'I'm quite happy to amuse myself.'

Before Hayley could stop her she'd wheeled herself across the room and entered Marcus's office.

Hayley jumped up quickly, almost spilling her tea on some finished letters, but by a miracle she righted her cup and mopped at the spilled drops with a tissue. That was all she needed now, to have to reprint an afternoon's work.

Determinedly, she crossed to Marcus's room, where the woman was busy looking through some files on his desk.

'What on earth do you think you're doing?' she demanded fiercely, and then caught sight of the smile cast over narrow shoulders.

'You're Audrey Blake, aren't you?' she said, her voice sounding annoyingly shaky from repressed temper. 'Why didn't you say so in the first place?'

'Because I wanted to see how long it would take you to guess,' she said triumphantly. 'Not very quick, are you, dear?'

Hayley felt goaded. 'Neither would you be, after a week like the last one.'

Audrey's smile didn't enhance her face, Hayley thought. No wonder the girls in the typing pool didn't like her. Her expression alone would put her to the bottom of any popularity poll.

'Finding it hard going, are you?' Audrey enquired with mock-concern. 'Well, don't worry. I'll be back on Monday to relieve you of the burden of *my* job.'

Hayley felt stunned. 'You're coming back to work on Monday?' She gasped in astonishment. 'Does Marcus know?'

Her brain was whirling. How could he do this to her, leaving it to the last minute to tell her? she thought with a surge of resentment.

'Not yet,' Audrey said. 'But he will, when I tell him.'

'Tell who what?'

Marcus's deep, pleasant voice startled them both. Two
flushed faces turned to him as he entered. He stopped
in the doorway in surprise.

'Good grief! Audrey! What on earth are you doing
here?'

He crossed the room and bent to kiss her thin cheek
as she beamed up at him.

'As I was just telling your *temp* here, after today her
services will no longer be required. On Monday I'll be
back.'

He frowned. 'A bit high-handed, even for you,
Audrey.'

Without looking at Hayley, he said, 'See if you can
get two coffees, will you? One black and one white.'

Hayley was fuming as she left the office. Irrationally,
most of her anger was for Marcus Maury, though she
could hardly expect him to tell Audrey she couldn't have
her job back, if she thought she was capable of doing
so. Still, her mutinous heart complained, he might have
just glanced at her, given her some moral support in a
moment when she had suffered such a body-blow. Didn't
he care that she would now have to leave him?

She groaned and stood still for a moment, with her
eyes closed, shocked by the strength of the emotions
which rocked her. It was the job she was leaving...the
job. It was her own idiotic fault if, somewhere along the
line, she had fused the job with the man. Stupidly, she
now felt as though she was losing both.

The office was filled with tension when Hayley returned with the coffee. Marcus was rubbing a deep
groove which had appeared between his eyes, and Audrey
was looking stubborn. They'd obviously stopped talking
as she'd entered, and didn't resume until she'd left and
closed the door behind her, a fact which didn't improve
her temper.

She rushed on furiously with her work in an attempt
to control the riot of her feelings, and had some sem-

blance of composure as the door to the inner office finally opened and Marcus came out, pushing Audrey in her wheelchair.

Hayley felt a heavy black cloud descend around her head.

He said matter-of-factly, 'I'm just taking Audrey home. Hold the fort. I'll be back.'

Audrey's eyes met hers with a look of triumph. 'Goodbyee!' she crooned sweetly. 'I hope you have lots of luck finding a new job.'

After they'd gone Hayley threw her half-eaten bun into the bin and rinsed her cup under the tap in the small basin in her office.

Her eyes felt dry and hot, which was preferable to tears, she thought gloomily. Perhaps a fresh cup of tea might help matters, because nothing else was going to.

She met Liz Jarvis in the corridor and groaned silently at the look of overt enjoyment on the blonde girl's face.

'Was that Audrey Blake I saw earlier?'

Liz invariably went for the jugular, Hayley thought with cynical amusement, but perhaps that was better than more usual veiled hints.

'Yes.'

Liz snorted. 'I thought it wouldn't be long. Once she saw what you looked like, ten broken legs wouldn't have kept her from scooting back.'

Hayley decided against pointing out that Audrey only had two.

'But Audrey's never seen me,' Hayley countered drily.

'Not in the flesh,' Liz agreed. 'But you can bet your best boots she saw the company mag. There's a picture of you in this month's issue, in glorious Technicolor, saying you were dreamboat's new secretary. No wonder she got her skates on, or should I say her wheel-chair wheels?'

Hayley ignored the cruel little joke, shaking her head in puzzlement. 'A picture of me? But where on earth would they get a picture of me?'

Liz shrugged. 'It's your mug shot, probably. You know, the one you had taken for your security tag.'

'But surely they would have asked me first?' Hayley said in utter astonishment. 'I might not have been agreeable.'

'During working hours you're company property, my dear,' Liz said cynically. 'And there isn't a thing you can do if they want to publish the fact.'

Hayley swallowed a peculiar little lump in her throat. 'I suppose not.' But her first appearance in print had certainly brought her bad luck, she mused gloomily.

Liz's mind was obviously running on similar lines.

'Still, it's bad luck it brought the fire-breathing dragon back before time.' She sounded genuinely sympathetic. 'She just couldn't take the risk of you succeeding where she'd failed. She must have reckoned that with looks like yours you'd have a head start. All you'd need would be time.'

'I'm afraid I don't follow.'

'Don't you?' Liz tilted her head disbelievingly. 'You don't seem dim to me, but I'll spell it out. She's in love with him. Has been for eight years. Not that it's got her anywhere. The man's got better taste.'

Hayley shook her head. 'But doesn't she know? He's got Felicity Braun.'

'And before her there was Lauretta Newson and before her Elise something or other. She knows he's never serious about his glamour girls. And every time one bites the dust she thinks she's in with a chance again.' She pulled a wry face. 'Some chance! There's no fool like a blind fool.'

Hayley thought grimly that that, at least, was true. She must try to remember it.

Liz said breezily, 'Has he given you the sack yet?'

Hayley gave a short, unamused laugh. 'Not yet. But no doubt he will when he gets back.'

But he wasn't back by five-fifteen, which was the time they finished on Friday. She sat at her desk, chewing her nails and trying not to keep going over in her mind all Liz Jarvis had told her.

There was one thing both Liz and Audrey were wrong about anyway, she thought ironically. Given any amount of time, there was little hope that Marcus Maury would ever see her as anything but an efficient machine, there simply to take some weight off his shoulders and to make life a little easier for him.

The occasional teasing and the kissing were little side-dishes to his meal of life. Something to add relish, but not to sustain. Unlike Audrey's, Hayley's eyes were wide open to that fact. No amount of time would make her a main dish.

And she could never be anything else. When and if she fell in love, it would be with a man who knew how to be faithful...if there was such a rare creature and she was lucky enough to find him.

But, whoever he was, he wasn't Marcus Maury, and it was time she understood that.

She tried not to dwell on the fact that he was with Audrey. Perhaps Liz wasn't as clued up as she thought. Perhaps there was, after all, something more substantial than hope that kept Audrey Blake hanging on.

By a quarter to six, the suspense was unbearable, and in a flash of temper she gathered up her belongings and left. She was going home, and if he wanted to give her the boot tonight he would have to elongate his foot that far, she thought rebelliously. Otherwise he would have to wait until Monday. Always supposing she turned up to face the final curtain.

The sunny day had faded into grey evening, a far more fitting backdrop for her present frame of mind, she thought morosely.

And, on top of everything else, she came out of the office building to find she'd just missed her bus, and, with a sigh of exasperation, she watched it trundling out of sight around the next corner.

Too restless to stand idly waiting for another, she began to walk on to the next stop, stepping out briskly in the hope of clearing her head.

She was standing on the corner of a side-street, waiting to cross, when a car drew into the kerb. The driver's window wound down.

'Here! Hayley! Get in and I'll drive you home.'

For a moment she stared blankly. Then, as she recognised Marcus, who was peering out at her, an irritable expression on his face, she shook her head.

'No, thanks. I'd rather not.'

Marcus Maury stared at her in surprise, then, as the lights changed and a horn blared behind him, he snapped, 'For heaven's sake, woman! I'm holding up the traffic. Get in! And that's an order.'

Hayley was tempted to tell him he no longer had the right to give her orders, but, seeing the thunderous descent of his brows, she walked around the bonnet and got into the passenger seat.

So he'd finally decided to come back, she thought, her anger still simmering. Did he think his ungracious offer of a lift home was sufficient to make up to her for her pain and disillusion?

Bordering on mild hysteria, she almost laughed aloud. Because he didn't know—how could he?—that she was suffering more than the disappointment of having lost her job.

Leaning back with her head against the rest, she let out a long, shaky breath.

Marcus drove on for a while before he said in an ironic tone, 'Are you going to tell me what all that was about?'

Hayley sat beside him, feeling the colour return to her pale cheeks, along with a surge of defiance.

'Nothing to tell. I just felt like a walk.'

He shot her a frowning sideways glance, but there was a hint of laughter in the vivid blue eyes.

'Audrey got under your skin, did she? Irritating other women is something she's good at, I agree.'

She said tightly, 'But she doesn't have the same effect on men, apparently.' Her mouth curled contemptuously. 'But then men rarely look beyond the obvious.'

He made a grim sound. 'I thought you promised me Miss Pushy was out of my life for good.'

She said, with a hint of bitterness, 'That was when I worked for you. Now I don't, we're on even ground. I can choose to be whom I please, and there's not a thing you can do about it.'

'Is that so?' His voice was deceptively soft, his darting glance alight with a challenge so intimate that it almost took her breath away. 'Does that mean I can indulge my own choices too?'

She shrugged. 'Certainly. As long as they don't involve me.'

He shot her a glance and then, without warning, pulled off the road and into the car park of a nearby inn. She stared at him in surprise and he laughed.

'I think you need a drink. It will help to calm your nerves.'

'But you're driving,' she protested.

He grinned, a sudden relaxed expression lighting his face, chasing the lines of tiredness away. 'I didn't say *my* nerves needed calming. I'll have a mineral water to keep you company while you have a brandy.'

As she opened her mouth to protest he placed his lips against hers in a light, brief kiss.

'No harassment intended,' he teased. 'Just a little gentle persuasion.'

As he got out to open her door for her she absently touched her fingers against her lips, which burned like the hottest flame. Feeling a little dizzy, she followed him

into the warm, pleasantly lit bar and allowed him to seat
her in a cosy alcove.

She thought unwillingly of Frank Heaton. How was
it some men could steal kisses without the least offence,
while others...?

She shuddered, and put Frank firmly out of her mind.

It helped to watch Marcus as he walked to the bar,
her volatile senses excited by the view of his tall, lithe
figure, moving easily, belying the dynamic vitality of him,
and she felt her pulses begin to race.

The magic he wove over her was as strong as her resistance was weak, she acknowledged with a feeling of
helplessness. Perhaps Audrey had turned up in the nick
of time after all. But she couldn't take consolation from
the thought.

Soon there would be no more of this daily heady excitement, she acknowledged miserably. And, like a
beggar at a feast, she let herself go on watching him,
drinking in every last detail of his powerful masculinity.

She had her head down, trying to control the rise of
colour her thoughts had released, as he came back towards her, carrying two glasses.

He was right. The brandy warmed her through and
she felt the tension gradually easing out of her body.

As they settled back into the comfortable alcove, she
stole a look at him and found that he was studying her
also. She looked away in confusion, and he laughed.

'No penalties for looking,' he said, gently mocking.

'I suppose not,' she muttered. Hadn't she been doing
the same thing herself only seconds ago? Although it
was doubtful if his thoughts were going in the same direction as hers.

'Now, then!' he began firmly, in a voice that caused
her to tense again.

Here it comes, the closing knell, she thought, with
a silent sigh of resignation. She steeled herself to
look unconcerned.

He gave her a direct look. 'Bring me up to date. Just when did you stop working for me?'

Her soft brown eyes widened in surprise. 'I'd have thought that was obvious! From the moment Audrey Blake walked back into her office, or should I say wheeled back?'

He ignored the intended humour, looking at her impatiently, as though expecting her to go on.

She said, somewhat irritably, 'Well, that's it, isn't it? The job was mine until she came back, you said. And now she's back.'

He shrugged. 'Have I given you notice?'

'Not yet. But of course you will.' Meeting his frowning look, she said, trying for nonchalance, 'It's all right. That was the arrangement, so I've no hard feelings.'

Except against fate and that damned photograph, she added silently. If it hadn't been for that, I might have had a few more weeks of... She caught herself up with a silent gasp. Hadn't she already decided Audrey turning up might be a blessing in disguise? Since otherwise she'd only end up making a fool of herself.

His blue eyes probed hers, as though searching for answers to unasked questions. His intensity started her heart banging again, and she wrenched her eyes away.

He seemed exasperated. 'Are you saying you'd be happy to go?'

She made a short, impatient sound. 'Not exactly happy... but not unprepared.'

Why was he holding an inquest on the situation? she wondered resentfully. Why couldn't he just get it over with and let the matter drop? Perhaps, in his conceit, he expected a few tears. She had a feeling she might shed a few later on... but not now.

He gave a short laugh. 'Don't you think you're jumping the gun a little? Audrey isn't coming back. At least, not yet.'

'Not coming back?' Hayley's heart gave a leap of pure joy. 'But I thought...'

'You thought,' he repeated with that enigmatic look that drove her wild. 'But not carefully enough, or you'd have realised that Audrey coming back now would be impossible.'

'Impossible?' She was confused.

'That's right. With all the merger meetings coming up, I need a secretary who is mobile. Audrey simply isn't up to it.'

A peculiar kind of pain was starting deep inside her, and she dug her nails into her palms. For one wild moment she had thought he had meant it would be impossible for him to let her go...

He was watching her carefully through narrowed lids, waiting for her reaction.

'Well? Are you interested in staying on?'

Hayley said, 'Can I think about it?'

He gave an amused laugh, the sound making Hayley's toes curl faintly. Everything about this man, she realised with a pang, seemed capable of drawing some response from her.

'How long would you need to think?'

Hayley began to feel like a condemned prisoner facing the possibility of a reprieve. A bubble of excitement was struggling to surface, but she pushed it firmly down.

'And when the mergers are over, what then?'

He shrugged. 'That won't be for a long time, if I'm any judge. Some of the take-overs look like being pretty messy. From here on in, things are likely to be chaotic. But I have a feeling we'll manage it together, don't you?'

A pulse began to beat in her throat as she struggled with her growing excitement. She wanted desperately to say yes, but found herself hanging back. The job itself would be only a minor challenge in comparison to the one she would have to set herself. Could she work that closely with him and not come to grief? It was time to

admit to herself that her feelings were already past the
stage of idle fascination and into something much deeper.
Which could lead her nowhere...except heartache.

And, if he ever found out, it would no doubt cause
him some amusement, she surmised. It wasn't the first
time his secretary had fallen in love with him. She had
a shrewd suspicion that more secretaries than Audrey
Blake had done her best with that one, and been dashed
against a rock.

'How did Audrey take the news?' she asked, hearing
the hint of bitchiness in her voice with dismay, but still
going on. 'Did you have to offer her your own unique
brand of consolation? Is that why you didn't bother to
come back to the office on time?'

For a moment he seemed disconcerted, then his well-
shaped mouth thinned into a cool smile. He said in a
clipped voice, 'She was disappointed, naturally, and I
was sorry. We've worked together for a long time, and
Audrey isn't one to enjoy being idle. But in the end she
understood.' His eyes probed Hayley's almost brutally.
'I was late back because of the usual peak-hour traffic.'
His blue gaze relented a little. 'Did you think I was
making love to Audrey?' he jeered softly. 'Do I seem
the type to take advantage of an invalid?'

Hayley felt her colour rise, and lowered her eyes in
acute embarrassment.

'No. Of course not. Why should I even think such a
thing?'

He shook his head in slow amusement. 'I can't imagine. But women are the strangest creatures, at the best
of times.'

Hayley groaned silently. Dear God! Had he really recognised the green emotion behind her gibes?

'I'm sorry. I didn't think of the traffic. I suppose I
was a bit strung up, thinking you were going to...'

She ground to a halt, aware that her voice had cracked.

'Dispense with your services?' he suggested gently.

She nodded. 'Something like that. I just wanted to get it over with.'

'Never a pleasant experience,' he agreed with a nod. 'But, now we've sorted out that little misunderstanding, do you feel a little better?'

She found it difficult to meet his eyes, still trying to define the tumult of her emotions. She was on dangerous ground, she knew, and would need to think things out very carefully before committing herself to what, for her, would be much more than just a job. Would she be able to cope with his magnetism...the feelings he already aroused and which could only grow stronger...?

She gave a silent gasp as she realised the trend of her thoughts. Good grief! That was *all* the man was offering her...a job, not a love-affair. She'd have no one to blame if she tried to read anything more into it. He hadn't asked her to stay on out of warm feelings for her...or a reluctance to see her go. He needed her...but only to keep the work wheels turning.

She heaved a sigh. 'As I said, I have to think about it.'

He nodded his head.

'OK. You do that. But I'd like your decision next time we meet.'

Which would be on Monday, she thought, feeling a little sad. Audrey's unexpected appearance had forced her to confront her real feelings about working for Marcus and brought a subtle change in their relationship. It marked the end of an era, and she wasn't at all sure she could cope with the beginning of the new one, whichever way it went.

CHAPTER SIX

ANTHEA called from her bedroom as Hayley came in the front door.

'Is that you, Hayley? I was getting worried.'

'You needn't have worried.' Hayley trailed in and sat on Anthea's bed, watching her apply, with a quick, sure hand, her flamboyant make-up. 'Why the war-paint?'

'I've got a date. His name's Lenny Barnes.' Anthea could still talk while lavishly applying her violet lipstick. 'I met him at a party more than a month ago. It's taken him this long to ring. He's taking me to dinner.'

Hayley sniffed the air. 'It's your turn to cook tonight. I don't suppose you've done anything.'

Anthea put the final coat of bright blue mascara to her lashes and turned away from the mirror.

'What do you think?'

She looked bright, colourful, brimming with life. Hayley, with a rush of affection, said, 'Incredible.'

'Thanks.' She patted Hayley's head on the way to the kitchen. 'I'll pop out and get you a Chinese, then I'll be off. Don't wait up.'

'Don't worry. I won't. I'm ready for an early night.'

Anthea regarded her as she stood in the doorway. 'You look a bit peaky. Are you all right? Why were you so late?'

'Pressure of work.' Too tired to discuss it, Hayley lied a little and waved a dismissive hand. 'I'll get into the shower in a minute. Then I'll eat my Chinese supper and have an early night. You just go off and enjoy yourself.'

Anthea didn't need too much coaxing. Her mind was full of Lenny Barnes, and the sparkle was back in her slate-blue eyes.

Hayley yawned, stretched her aching limbs, and looked at the clock, deciding there was time for a long, leisurely shower before Anthea returned with the supper. The takeaway would be full at this hour, and she'd probably have to wait for quite a while.

Standing under the warm, soothing jet of water, Hayley felt the tension beginning to ease out of her body. The smooth, silky feel of the soap against her skin was like the lightest touch, and suddenly she was thinking of Marcus Maury again, remembering how, that night when she'd locked herself in, his hands had run over her body, exciting, arousing, creating a tremor along her nerves ...

The sound of the front door brought her out of her reverie with a guilty start. Anthea was back with the food, and suddenly Hayley was hungry.

She quickly shampooed and rinsed her hair and reached for the towel, which she normally hung on the rail outside the shower curtain, only now there wasn't one there.

'Damn!' She swore irritably. 'Why didn't I find one *before* I got wet?' She raised her voice. 'Anthea! I'm in the shower and I need a towel.'

While she waited, she wrung the moisture out of her long, thick hair and blinked the water from her eyes, wondering what was taking Anthea so long. Perhaps she hadn't heard the front door after all, she thought, and groaned. Now she would have to find the towel herself.

With an impatient gesture, she pulled the curtain aside and stepped out on to the bath-mat, just as Marcus Maury entered with a bath-towel in his hand.

He stopped, only feet away, his eyes widening a little, and then a slow smile spread across his face.

'Sorry to be so long,' he said casually. 'It took me a while to find the linen cupboard.'

Frozen with surprise and shock, Hayley stood and dripped water from her slender curves on to the bath-mat, while his eyes moved over her slowly from head to toe, with an expression that was easily recognisable.

'Hayley,' he said softly, with a little shake of his head, 'You're spectacular.'

Returning suddenly to life, she leaned forward and grabbed the towel from his hand, turning her back to wrap it around her, huddling into its warmth as she shivered from reaction.

'But not, however, a public spectacle,' she ground furiously, keeping her face turned from him, hiding the flush of anger mixed with excitement. 'Would you mind leaving the bathroom so that I can dress?'

He gave a low laugh that seemed to echo through her nervous system in a series of tremors.

'Not a word of thanks,' he said reproachfully. 'But since I'm here ... would you like a hand to wipe?'

'No! Please get out!'

His very presence spelled danger, but the real danger lay deep in her heart, with every second a threat to her composure, every pulse-beat a moment nearer surrender. If he should touch her ...

He didn't answer, and there was no sound.

The silence frayed Hayley's nerves almost to breaking-point. Where was he? What was he doing?

Risking a quick glance over her shoulder, she saw he was moving towards her, and, with a gasp, she half turned, backing away, feeling the raised slippery tiles of the shower cubicle against her foot. She stumbled blindly for a moment, still holding grimly on to the towel, before feeling his hands grip her arms to steady her.

The touch of his hands against her bare skin was like a burning brand, sending spears of heat shooting through her body.

She was suddenly frightened, not knowing what she feared. 'Let go of me!'

'Easy! Easy!' he soothed, drawing her towards him as she began to pull away. Then, seeing the glint of panic in her wide brown eyes as she stared up at him, he tutted softly. 'Great heavens, Hayley! I'm not here to molest you.'

Through teeth she'd clenched to stop them from chattering, she managed to say harshly, 'Then why are you here?'

He *was* molesting her, she thought wildly. He was here, in her bathroom, holding her in a way, and with a look in his eyes, that would have had her screaming if he'd been any other man. But, because it was him, what he seemed to be offering was a promise of heaven.

But she knew better than to take it. The result would be the same, whoever the man, in this situation... an opportunistic moment of passion. In the aftermath she would inevitably suffer rejection, humiliation, ultimate self-disgust.

'Answer me!' she insisted in a voice that shook, despite her efforts to appear in charge of herself. 'Or is the answer too obvious?'

'I came back,' he began, his blue eyes still holding the warmth of amusement, 'to return your handbag, which you left in my car.'

Hayley's hard gaze faltered and became embarrassment. 'Oh!' Then suspiciously, 'But how did you get in? Anthea isn't here.'

'I know. Or at least I guessed, since the front door was left ajar, that someone had just popped out.' He shook his head. 'A dangerous thing to do. Especially since you were in the shower.' And then, with a touch of irony, 'Anyone could have come in.'

'Someone did!' Hayley said accusingly. 'Why didn't you just wait in the living-room?'

'I did. But you called for a towel. So I brought you one, though I didn't expect you to get out of the shower to thank me.' He grinned down at her, his eyes seeming to devour her flushed, angry face with every evidence of enjoyment. 'But I'm glad you did.'

Her eyes flashed with anger. 'I might have guessed you'd enjoy a peep show.'

He smiled, his head tilted to one side. 'Except I didn't have to peep. You were there, an arm's length away, in all your remarkable glory.' His smile widened tauntingly. 'It's times like these that I'm glad I have a photographic memory.'

He was too close. Overpoweringly so. Hayley felt the discomfort of his magnetic vitality, and tired to extricate herself.

'OK! Well, you've had your joke.' The heat in her cheeks seemed to have reached the point of combustion. 'So would you leave now, please?'

He didn't release her immediately, but slowly brushed the wet hair from her cheek to hook it behind her ear.

His cool fingers were tantalising against her skin, and her chest heaved as her temper rose, disturbing the folds of the towel. 'Go!' she commanded.

As though drawn there irresistibly, his gaze settled momentarily on the cleavage revealed by the displaced towel, and then, with an air of bracing himself, he turned away with a sigh.

'I'll wait for you in the living-room.'

'There's no need to waste any more of your time,' she said edgily to his retreating back. 'Just leave my bag and...thanks.'

He gave a dismissive little wave. 'My pleasure.' His tone was mocking, giving his words a double meaning which wasn't lost on Hayley. He stood in the doorway for a last glance, before giving another sigh. 'Don't be long.'

Hayley seethed as she rubbed herself dry. She still tingled from head to foot, as though his roving glance had been an exploring hand...the same hand she had been imagining in the shower, to the accompaniment of such delicious sensations that just remembering them had her burning with shame.

As he'd said, he'd been an arm's length away, and
there had been a brief moment, a vivid flash, when she'd
thought, perhaps hoped, he was, despite her protests,
going to bridge the gap and make her fantasies reality.
Was it possible he might have done, if she hadn't broken
the spell? An unanswerable question, but her heart
bumped unevenly at the thought.

It was hard to believe he was the same demanding
man who had been briskly dictating letters to her earlier
in the day. In the office, cool and authoritative, he was
daunting, but at least she knew where she stood. This
taunting, teasing side of his nature didn't surface very
often, but when it did she found herself almost inevitably on the losing side. More approachable, but dis-
mayingly unpredictable, he was even more of an enigma.
And more, much more of a danger to her self-control.

With the towel still clutched about her, she risked a
peek out into the hallway and, finding it empty, dashed
across it to her bedroom shutting the door firmly behind
her. She took her time dressing and drying her hair,
giving him plenty of time to leave.

He was hovering about the stove when she eventually
emerged.

Hayley stood open-mouthed in dismay. 'I thought
you'd gone.'

'No. I was just about to pop the take-away in the oven
to keep warm, but I haven't yet decided how the cooker
works.'

'Don't bother. I'll do it later. After you've gone.' She
looked around a little wildly. 'Where's Anthea?'

He shrugged. 'I've no idea.'

'But she went for the take-away. You must have been
here when she came back.'

'Uh huh!' He shook his head, a glint of amusement
warming his blue eyes. 'The food was here when I arrived, but no Anthea.'

Hayley bit her lip in vexation. The scatter-brained idiot must have dashed in and dashed straight out again, leaving the front door standing ajar. It tended to do that unless you gave it a good slam.

Anthea had gone and wouldn't be back for hours—if at all! She was here in the flat all alone with Marcus Maury, who seemed to be in a very strange mood.

She said pointedly, 'Well, thanks again for returning my bag.'

'Don't mention it.' He'd managed to light the cooker and was putting the foil containers into the oven. 'We share a liking for Chinese food, it seems. Would you care to thank me a little more substantially by letting me share this with you? There's more than enough for two.'

She made a derisive sound. 'I should have thought your taste would run to something a little more exotic.'

'It does . . . sometimes.' The pause seemed significant. 'And sometimes I enjoy the wholesome taste of home cooking.' That peculiar smile was playing about his mouth, drawing Hayley's fascinated gaze and playing havoc with her heartbeat.

For some reason she thought of what Liz had said about him tiring of his glamour girls, and Audrey's hopeless hope that he would turn eventually to her.

Hayley queried in silent bitterness, Is that what I am? A wholesome taste? Is that why you're here tonight? To clear your palate for your rarer dishes?

'Into which category does a Chinese take-away fall?' she asked, with an edge of sarcasm.

'Ah!' He looked annoyingly pensive. 'Chinese take-aways are something else again. They remind me of my student days, spent in a flat very much like this one.'

He had seated himself at the small dining-table, and she felt foolish standing, as though she were the visitor and he the resident, quite at home. He'd taken the outside seat, and she had to squeeze past him to sit. He made a little sound of appreciation as her body pressed mo-

mentarily against his, and she wondered, a little resentfully, if he'd planned it that away.

But at least, seated beside him, she wouldn't have to
look directly at him, and he wouldn't see the effect of
his nearness reflected in her expressive face.

'I just can't imagine you in a rented flat,' she said,
interested despite her irritation. 'Somehow I'd imagined
you'd been born with a silver spoon in your mouth.'

He laughed. 'I was, but my grandfather promptly removed it on the day I joined the company. He believed
in old-fashioned notions like getting out on your own
and working your way up in life—literally, from the
bottom. He also thought hard work and adversity forged
character.'

'Well, there's plenty of both in my life,' Hayley con-
tributed ruefully, wondering how much forging had been
done on her character. 'And I suppose a flat like this
could be described as the bottom.'

She glanced critically about the cramped little kitchen,
which was nothing more than a corner of the living-
room, separated by a built-in room divider. Not that the
flat was squalid. Despite her somewhat slapdash attitude to life, Anthea had made the place bright and
comfortable.

'Maybe. But also a lot of fun.' A strangely nostalgic
look came into his startling blue eyes.

For some reason his far-away look and the smile
playing about his sensuous mouth annoyed Hayley, and
she wondered, with an odd disconsolation, what kind
of women had accompanied his rise up each rung of the
ladder to the top. Even more oddly, she found herself
wanting to break into the memories that were putting
that look on his face.

'More fun, I should think, when it's automatically
guaranteed the silver spoon will be there waiting, no
matter what,' she scorned.

The sudden chill in the air was almost tangible, and Hayley felt herself turning pale as he caught her in a narrowed, icy stare.

'Nothing automatic about it, Miss Morgan. I worked for what I have—with my best effort.' His smiling mouth was now a grim line. 'Which is why I accept nothing less from my employees.'

She'd been wrong, Hayley knew, goaded by jealousy of a past that was his by right, and none of her business.

She bit her lip and mumbled her apology. 'I'm sorry.'

He dismissed it with a wave of his hand and rose from the rather rickety table, made festive by Anthea's best cloth.

'I think that food should be warm enough now.'

She stared up at him. 'If you'd prefer to leave, I wouldn't mind.'

'But I would.'

To her surprise he bent and kissed her mouth, the amusement back in his blue eyes.

'I'm starving! And I don't intend to let a little difference of opinion rob me of my just deserts.'

He took plates from the cupboard and put them in the oven to warm after he'd removed the foil containers. Lifting the lids, he sniffed appreciatively. 'Chicken chow mein. My favourite.'

Hayley watched him filling the plates, her eyes on the lithe movements of his body. He'd removed his jacket and tie, and she could see the play of hard, flexible muscle beneath the snowy cotton of his shirt as he absorbed himself in the task of judicious sharing.

He was a man at home in any situation, she realised with an odd pang, equally in command whether issuing orders from behind his imposing desk, or presiding at the kitchen stove. She had a sudden, unnerving picture of them living together in domestic bliss with a lifetime of cosy evenings before them, and was almost overcome by a fluttering weakness.

Making no attempt to help him, she let him set the meal before her, eating in a detached way, satisfying one hunger as another grew.

With his shirt-sleeves rolled up to the elbows and his thick red-brown hair slightly tousled, he was even more devastating.

She watched the play of expressions across his strong, handsome face as he talked, the glint of humorous enjoyment in the bright blue eyes, only half listening as he regaled her with tales of flats with faulty plumbing and miserly landlords who ignored holes in rotten floorboards and windows that couldn't be shut, and dark, cold winter nights of endless study, and long, lazy summer days spent mostly on the river.

A strange, bitter-sweet yearning began and expanded inside Hayley until it became a pain. It was like looking into a brightly lit shop window, knowing the wonderful, desirable things displayed there were beyond her reach. And she was suddenly angry.

He was back at the stove, making coffee from the instant granules in the jar, whistling tunelessly beneath his breath.

'Marcus,' she said harshly, 'why are you here?'

He turned around to look at her, his brows drawn over narrowed eyes that were a smoky blue. 'Don't you know?'

She was suddenly breathless. 'No.'

'Then I'll tell you.' He turned off the gas flame and moved swiftly to sit beside her. 'Or better still, I'll show you.'

He gripped her shoulders, drawing her forwards so that her face was close to his. For the first time she realised that, in choosing to sit where she had, she'd hemmed herself in with no avenue of escape.

But the darkened intensity of his gaze had her mesmerised, and even if she could have done she would have made no move. And he could glimpse his victory in her wide, velvet-soft eyes.

A triumphant little smile curved his mouth just before it descended to claim her own, parting her lips hungrily. After only a brief, automatic tensing, she relaxed. As though waiting for that signal, his kiss deepened, lengthened into a drugging sweetness.

She felt a tremendous urge to touch him, and brushed her fingers tentatively against his cheek, feeling his jaw clench beneath the firm, smooth skin, hearing the sharp intake of his breath.

His arms closed tightly around her, almost crushing her with their strength, and his kiss became fiercely possessive, searching for and finding a matching passion. His mouth lifted suddenly to begin an exploration of her closed lids, then her ears, his tongue flicking against the delicate lobes...a sensation that had her gasping. Remorselessly his lips burned a path down the arched curve of her throat, resting against the pulse beating frantically in the hollow.

Her fingers slid into the thick, clean hair, clinging as though to a lifeline, as undreamt-of sensations rocked her. Somewhere, on another plane, she was soaring, but there was more...so much more that she needed, with an aching intensity. If only she knew what it was.

'Marcus. Oh, Marcus.' Huskily she murmured his name, willing him to solve the mystery.

He growled deep in his throat. The crushing hold loosened and his hand touched against her throat, and brushed away the soft fabric of her blouse, baring her shoulder to his lips, which blazed a white heat against her skin. Buttons slid open to the touch of his long, lean fingers, revealing the aroused thrust of her breasts. He stopped kissing her to gaze at what lay bared, and slowly his hand caressed her, his darkly smouldering eyes lifting to hers, where no secrets remained.

'Hayley.' He murmured her name raggedly. 'My sweet girl. If only you knew how much...'

He was shaking his head, his expression almost sorrowful. He seemed to be moving away from her, the distance growing alarmingly.

Hayley reached out and drew him back, her lips fastening on his, her hand covering the fingers which still lay against her breast. Her whole body burned with a feverish heat, trembled with a hungry desire that had her arching against him.

He moaned and slid his arms about her, enveloping her in a gentle hold. His lips softened, the heat of passion receding as her trembling grew. Then he took his mouth away and pressed it against her cheek, whispering her name over and over against its softness.

It was over, she knew with a sick sense of loss. Heaven had slipped from her grasp, but she couldn't withdraw from him.

It was he who gently disentangled himself from her, pulling her blouse over her breasts, and brushing her tumbled hair from her face, before tenderly cupping it between both his hands.

His eyes, still smouldering faintly in the ashes of passion, held hers steadily.

She gazed back in confusion, and said, like a sleepwalker returning to consciousness, 'What happened?'

'Looks as if we both got a little carried away.' His deep voice held a tremor. He smiled and waited for her trembling response before giving a deep sigh and dropping his hands.

He was back at the stove, reheating the kettle. His shoulders tensed and bunched as though with the remnants of emotion, and Hayley realised, with a little sense of shock, that he was nothing like as calm as he had appeared.

She drew a little sobbing breath and said haltingly, her voice full of hurt and anger, 'Did I f-fail some kind of...test?'

His hands gripped the edge of the sink, and it was some seconds before he turned. There was a wry twist to his mouth.

'No. The test was for me, and *I* almost failed.'

'I don't understand.'

He shook his head with a sharp movement, like a dog dislodging an annoying fly.

'Perhaps it's better that way.'

He didn't finish his coffee, seeming suddenly anxious to leave.

Hayley felt the same anxiety for him to be gone, so that she could examine her feelings, which were tumultuous...confused...a mixture of relief and awful humiliation. Had she been saved? Or rejected? Had she shown him too clearly how she'd felt about him and frightened him off? The sex he could take with equanimity. But perhaps now that he had recognised the feelings behind it, which she'd displayed all too obviously, it might have become an altogether different situation.

As she rose to see him out he paused, looking down into her face with a worried frown between his brows. Hayley found it difficult to meet his gaze and dropped her head, letting her thick hair hide the riot of her feelings.

'Are you still working for me?' The question was unexpected and almost hesitant, and surprised her into looking up again.

She felt a sharp stab of indignation. It hadn't taken him long to come down to earth...back to the really *important* issues.

'I don't know. I haven't had long enough to think,' she said at last. 'You said to answer by Monday.'

'I said the next time we met,' he insisted doggedly.
'So do you want the job?'

Hayley felt an almost hysterical urge to laugh.
Nothing's changed, she thought, a little ray of light
piercing her gloom. Like this—irritable and persistent—
she could handle him.

She said in a burst of exasperation, 'Well, yes, I do.
But I can't imagine why you still want me.'

The answer he gave her was one which shouldn't have
surprised her. His reasoning was the same as it had
always been.

'I want a competent secretary to help me finish up the
job of the mergers, preferably you, since you already
know something of the work.' He grimaced. 'But if
you're not sure...'

She was beginning to feel like a cat with nine lives.
Each time he gave her a fresh start, she somehow
managed to muck it up. But here he was giving her
another chance. All in his own best interests, of course,
but a chance none the less. It might be possible, after
all, to paste back the pieces of her pride.

'I'm sure,' she said, with a feeling that she had
managed to grasp something that had been slipping
swiftly through her fingers. 'Absolutely sure.'

'Then that's settled.' He nodded in satisfaction.
'Good!'

That, it seemed, was the end of the conversation, so
Hayley led the way through the short passageway and
opened the front door, standing aside to let him out. As
he passed she impulsively took his arm, and he turned
to look down at her.

Hardly knowing why she'd detained him, she was momentarily at a loss for words, then she said, in a low
voice, 'Marcus, will tonight cause a problem?'

His broad chest rose and fell in a sigh. 'No problem,'
he said with a wintry little smile. 'I suppose it's just been
one of those days.'

Her hand was still on his arm, her fingers curved against the hard muscle, and he looked down and then took it in his, lifting it slowly, turning the palm to his mouth in a brief kiss that curled her toes and made her glad she was leaning against the door.

As he moved away she said, sounding husky, 'Thanks for returning my handbag.'

'That's OK.' She saw the gleam of his smile. 'The memorable view alone was well worth the trouble.'

CHAPTER SEVEN

MARCUS, though friendly, had definitely reconstructed the barriers. In a way it was a relief, since Hayley hadn't quite known what attitude to expect from him.

His visit to the flat to return her handbag had served him a dual purpose, the most urgent of which, it appeared, had been to make sure of her agreement to go on doing the job of secretary.

Had the lovemaking been something else, or part of a plan of persuasion? From his present demeanour, she would never know. And he would never know how close he'd come to defeating his object. Perhaps that was just as well.

If they'd gone on to make love, she could never have worked for him again, and they would each have been the loser.

The extra work brought by the mergers was mounting daily, which kept him in the office far more, taking a greater share of the work which was rightfully hers.

Felicity came and went far more quickly these days, the periods behind the closed door of Marcus's office growing shorter. The pouting, provocative smile seemed to be wearing a little thin, Hayley thought, but perhaps that was just wishful thinking. The thinning line of her mouth these days showed grim determination rather than defeat.

And she still rang often, demanding to speak to Marcus, and was never refused. As Hayley put the calls through she heard the warmth of Marcus's greeting, and felt the powerful sword-thrust of jealousy which hung like a cloud for hours afterwards.

But, much to Hayley's secret delight, a closer rapport seemed to be building between Marcus and herself. He apparently now viewed her more as an assistant than a secretary and often sought and considered her opinion, but, if anything, he was even more careful to keep his distance.

He came into her office one morning, bringing Martin Lukes to introduce him to Hayley.

'Martin is part of the small management team I've set up to co-ordinate the finances of the mergers,' Marcus explained.

Hayley looked up and smiled, having no trouble recognising the blond young man who had startled her on her first day at one of the initial merger meetings. And he just as obviously remembered her.

'We should be seeing quite a bit of each other over the next few months.' He shook her hand warmly and grinned. 'I still can't believe my luck. And to think I'll get paid as well.'

Marcus's smile faded a little. He said ironically, 'Let's hope you still feel lucky when you see the amount of work involved. I don't think you'll have much time to spare for flirtation with Miss Morgan.'

Hayley shot him a surprised glance, wondering why he'd felt it necessary to issue the unsubtle warning. She was beginning, at last, to gain some perspective on Frank Heaton's behaviour, and felt in no danger from the friendly young accountant. She wished Marcus had left it to her to give any warnings that might become necessary. She was half tempted to make a note to mention it to him later, until she saw his face. He was obviously in no mood to be tackled today—not even diplomatically.

Martin Lukes coloured faintly under the cool, steady gaze of the blue eyes.

'No offence intended,' he said, sounding embarrassed. 'Just my idea of a joke.'

Marcus grimaced. 'Keep them for after working hours.'

Some of the frost remained in his voice as he said to Hayley, 'Make a start on the list of meetings to be arranged. I'll be back after lunch to discuss them.'

He left without a hint of the smile she'd grown accustomed to receiving, making her wonder how she'd managed to earn a share of his irritation.

He came back later, less irascible.

'With the exception of one, which should be here in a day or so, I've finally had all of the reports,' he said with a sigh of satisfaction. 'Now we can begin to tie up the loose ends.'

He put a number of files on her desk and sat down. 'Fit them in with the rest in the schedule for next week and begin arranging the meetings.'

Hayley frowned. 'I don't think we'll get them all into one week. Some of the companies are quite a distance away, and travelling will take up a lot of time.'

He said bracingly, 'Do your best. It might be worth while staying away from home a couple of nights to cut time and save going over the same ground more than once.'

Hayley gave a little gasp and looked directly up at him, momentarily distracted by the handsome lines of the face she had come to love. She wished, with a painful tug at her heart-strings, that she could see some answering interest in his expression. But there was only wry amusement.

He cast her an ironic glance from beneath thick brown lashes, causing her heart to stumble once or twice as her velvet-brown eyes became meshed in his clear blue gaze.

'Any problems with that?'

Hayley swallowed and dragged her mind back to what he had said. 'I . . . I don't think . . . so.'

'You don't sound convinced.' His brows lowered into a frown. 'Hayley! *Is* there a problem?'

The question was specific, she knew. What answer was he expecting?

She shook her head. 'None that I can think of.'

Except that she'd be with him somewhere, staying overnight, probably eating dinner, maybe even sleeping in adjoining rooms, which could become another form of agony if she allowed her imagination to run riot.

'Don't you think you can trust me?' he asked, surprising her with the gentleness of the query.

She coloured and bit her lip, finding herself unable to meet the unexpected warmth in his eyes. 'Of course.'

He nodded, and said a little ironically, 'Well, thanks for that, anyway.'

Hayley wondered what his reaction would be if he knew the real question was—could she trust herself?

With a hint of sudden and inexplicable malice she asked, 'Do you think Miss Braun will understand?'

His eyes narrowed, making them unreadable. 'Why shouldn't she? This is, after all, merely business.'

That's put me in my place, Hayley thought wryly. Which was the same place as that occupied by any other piece of office equipment . . . where it would be most useful! He couldn't have put it more plainly.

'So it is,' she agreed, forcing a smile. 'Shall we leave the long-distance meetings to the last? Or will it interfere with any weekend plans you and Miss Braun might have?'

'I shouldn't think so,' he said. 'After this weekend Felicity isn't going to be around for a while. She's beginning a new film.'

Hayley bit her lip to stop herself smiling.

He gave her a look that had her wondering uncomfortably whether he could read her mind, and his unexpected smile showed the glint of white teeth. 'So arrange them any way you like. I'm all yours.'

*   *   *

Marcus seemed withdrawn and a little cool as, the following Monday, they set out for the first in the series of meetings.

Hayley, seated in the front passenger seat of his roomy limousine, wondered at the breathlessness that overtook her as he settled himself in beside her.

He was a big man, and his broad shoulders, hard-muscled but not heavy, brushed against hers as he fastened his seat belt. His aura filled the confined space, making her almost dizzy with its headiness.

Almost as an afterthought, he turned to make sure she had fastened her belt, and made a soft tutting sound of impatience as he discovered her sitting as though lost in a dream.

Her breathlessness became near-suffocation as he leaned across her to fasten her belt. His handsome head was close to hers, his thick red-brown hair brushing lightly against her cheek, creating eddies of guilty sensation which coursed through her sensitised nerves and made her wonder how he could fail to be aware of her disturbance.

Lost in her study of the intriguing nape of his neck, she must have leaned towards him, for as his head came up it caught her chin a glancing blow, hard enough to bring the tears to her eyes and cause her head to snap back against the headrest.

'God! Hayley, I'm sorry!' He turned to cup her face in both his hands, looking worriedly into her eyes.

She met his appalled blue gaze in a kind of haze, felt his fingers touching tenderly against her smarting chin, brushing the shocked tears from her cheeks, and grew weak, her body slumping against the leather seat.

'You're not going to faint on me, are you?' he asked anxiously. 'Lord! What a clumsy idiot I am. I could have knocked you out.'

Painfully aware that it was more her fault than his, she felt embarrassed by his apology. Rousing herself, with an effort, she brushed his hands away, unable to bear the unnerving sensations he was creating.

'It was only a bump. I'll survive.' Her voice sounded thick and strange, muffled by the faint buzzing in her ears. 'If you'll give me a minute to recover.'

He released the seatbelts and drew her towards him, resting her head in the hollow of his shoulder. 'Take as long as you want.'

For a second she stiffened, in response to the fear which hadn't quite vanished. And now there was a new fear: that of letting him see again her stark need of him.

Involuntarily she tried to pull away, but with a soft sound of exasperation he drew her head back against his chest, where she lay listening to the strong rhythm of his heart, which seemed to beat a little faster as she nestled against him.

The warm comfort of his arms was a thrill, but one she knew would become a torment if prolonged. After a few moments, reluctantly, she withdrew.

He looked down at her questioningly. 'Feeling better?'

She smiled inwardly, ironically aware that there were two answers to that question. Yes and no. Not trusting herself to speak, she answered him with a nod.

'Am I permitted to see the damage?' He tilted her chin with a gentle finger, careful not to hurt. His face was close and she saw the thick lashes fanned across his lean cheeks as he peered closely. 'Hmm. You'll be lucky not to have a bruise.'

He dipped his head, and Hayley felt the touch of his lips against her chin. She gave a little gasp and unthinkingly put her hand softly against his cheek. He made a sharp sound and his eyes captured hers, almost drowning her in the depth of blue, reminding her of that other time she had looked into them like this.

Her lips parted on a sigh, smothered by the sudden touch of his mouth against hers as he kissed her lightly, undemandingly, giving her a chance to pull away if she

wished. But she didn't. Her will-power seemed to have
deserted her, sapped by the familiar yearning sensations
that stirred her deeply. The touch of his mouth was
warm, soft, almost tender. It took her breath away, and
when he lifted his head eventually she was speechless.

'Not a soothing poultice,' he said with a grin. 'But
the best I can do in the circumstances. Let me know if
you need a second application.'

Suddenly her breath returned, and with it a touch of
irritation. 'Sometimes, Marcus Maury. . .' she said with
asperity, and then stopped, lost for words to convey the
mixture of her feelings for him.

'I know. You could hate me.' He touched the tip of
her nose with a light finger. 'But the girl loves me really.'

It was said lightly, teasingly, and he wasn't even
looking at her as he fixed his seatbelt again. If he had,
he might have seen her stricken look and been in no
doubt that his joke had hit the nail painfully on the head.

As it turned out, it wasn't an entirely happy week, with
Marcus at his most irascible, wearing Hayley's patience
almost threadbare. The easy rapport which had become
established between them seemed to have vanished into
thin air, to be replaced by an uncomfortable tension, an
awareness that vibrated uneasily in the air, making it
almost impossible to relax in his company.

He drove her home in the evenings in almost total
silence, his gaze turned directly ahead, appearing deep
in thought, frowns of irritation forming and reforming
on his brow, following the obvious trend of his thoughts.

Hiding her sighs, Hayley gazed out of the window,
catching a glimpse now and then of her own reflection
revealed against the changing shades of the landscape.
The bruise had developed on her chin, and, fingering it
absently, she wondered if she had imagined the tender
moments of his remorse.

The negotiations were difficult, she knew, and some of the personalities involved made diplomacy almost impossible, but she'd seen him in trickier situations and admired his calm self-assurance. She wished he'd snap out of it, whatever it was, and found herself, at odd moments, irritated almost beyond endurance.

He was more demanding than ever, expecting her to anticipate his every need before he'd even spoken it, turning irritable if she disappeared from his side for more than a few minutes, yet making her feel almost invisible when she was there.

Hayley was grateful for the lunchtime respites, when Marcus was whisked off by other company executives and she was left to unwind over a sandwich and a cup of tea from the company canteen.

Martin Lukes attended the meetings, a friendly face in a sea of strangers. They ate lunch together when he was free, and strolled outside in the fresh air until it was time to resume the afternoon sessions. His good-natured flirting helped to redress the balance.

Wednesday morning's meeting proved another difficult one, and it was the nearest Hayley had come to losing her temper.

'I just don't know what's the matter with him,' she grumbled to Martin, breaking one of her cardinal rules of never discussing her employer. 'He's like a bear with a sore head.'

'He's probably seen this morning's paper,' Martin said with an amused grin. 'Looks like that actress girlfriend of his, Felicity something or other, might have given him the push. There's a picture of her out with someone else. Her new leading man or director or something.'

Hayley's heart lurched uncomfortably. Her first emotion was sympathy for Marcus, closely followed by a sneaking elation and then denial.

'Those kind of pictures don't mean a thing,' she said, more forcefully than she'd intended, since the elation shamed her. 'It's probably just publicity for the new film she's doing.'

Who are you trying to convince? she asked herself silently, relieved because some nicer part of herself hoped it was true. And yet a bust-up with Felicity was a very feasible explanation for his uncharacteristic behaviour of the past few days.

'Perhaps you should try telling the boss that,' Martin said flippantly, his smile fading a little as his eyes fixed on something over her shoulder. 'At the moment he looks as though he could do with some cheering up.'

She turned in the direction of his gaze and saw Marcus coming towards them, his expression grim.

'If I might interrupt,' he said caustically, his hard ice-blue gaze flicking over Hayley's flushed and inexplicably guilty face before settling on Martin. 'I want to go through these figures of yours before we begin this afternoon's session. Perkins seems to think they hold a number of errors.'

The following day Martin wasn't about, and in answer to her tentative enquiry Marcus informed her brusquely, 'He's doing what he should have done in the first place. His homework.'

On the way home in the car he surprised her with an invitation to dinner. Actually, it was more of a command than an invitation, and Hayley found herself meekly agreeing.

'Yes. Thank you. That would be nice.'

Silently she thought that if the past few days were anything to go on it would probably be far from nice.

To her surprise his face broke into a smile that, for the first time in what seemed a long time, actually reached his eyes, and she sighed with relief.

When she thought about it later, after he'd dropped her back at the flat, she felt annoyed. Did this dinner invitation, dropped on her from out of the blue, have

anything to do with Felicity Braun's rather public new
love-affair?

Despite what Liz Jarvis had said, the actress had
seemed to be still very much in his life. There'd been
little sign that he was getting bored—quite the opposite
in fact—and it was still possible this was one glamour
girl who might eventually make it with him to the altar.
The thought was painful ... very painful indeed.

An even more painful thought occurred. Was she being
used as a means of bring Felicity back to heel? Gloomily
she thought it very likely, and she was angry all over
again.

Nevertheless, sorting through her wardrobe, she felt
a tremor of anticipation.

As her hand slid back and forth along the rail it rested
on one of her few extravagances, a sheer silk blouse in
a delicate shade of turquoise, with a tiny matching
camisole, which suggested much but gave little away. The
colour turned her silky skin translucent, and, matched
with a softly swirling skirt of a deeper shade, it ensured
she'd stand out in almost any crowd.

She fixed filigree silver pendants into her ears and a
silver chain, inset with tiny pearls, about the creamy skin
of her slender throat, and surveyed the result in her
mirror with some satisfaction.

Her thick, dark hair, brushed until it gleamed, curled
softly about her neat head. Her velvet-brown eyes shone
clear and bright, and the faint flush of colour on her
cheeks added a natural glow. Once—a lifetime ago, it
seemed now—he had asked for glamour. Tonight she
would give it to him, with a vengeance.

But did she dare? After all, he had given her no idea
of the kind of dinner it was to be, and she wondered, a
little grimly, if she should pop a notebook and pencil
into her handbag, just in case.

Anthea was out again with Lenny Barnes. Hayley had been relieved at first, but wished now that her friend was here to give her her usual forthright opinion.

When Marcus arrived promptly at eight-thirty she sighed with relief. She hadn't made a mistake. He was dressed to kill. On anyone else the silver-grey suit, with paler grey silk shirt and slate-blue and grey tie, might have appeared sober, but on him it set just the right kind of understated background for his remarkable good looks.

Hayley felt suddenly shy, as though she were meeting him for the first time and had difficulty meeting his gaze. But when she did, the expression on his face took her breath away.

His eyes, after the initial flicker of surprise, darkened in unmistakable appreciation, and a soft whistle sounded through his teeth.

'Stunning!' he pronounced, bending to brush her lips lightly with his.

She moved jerkily away from him, reaching for a short jacket which she draped quickly about her shoulders.

'I'm ready. Shall we go?'

The admiration was still there in his eyes, and a smile slowly widened the sensuous mouth.

'I've never been more ready.'

Taking her hand and tucking it into the crook of his arm, he said, his voice sounding slightly husky, 'And I shall never have been more envied!'

Hayley wished she could believe he meant it, but she didn't dare. The inevitable disillusion would be too much to bear.

Marcus hailed a taxi to take them into town, leaving his car at the kerb in front of the flat.

'It's easier than trying to park in the centre,' he said in answer to her enquiring look.

Hayley's pulse increased. He would have to accompany her back to the flat, which would be empty,

as it had been every other night that Anthea had been
out on a date with Lenny Barnes. Having met Lenny
once or twice, Hayley wasn't sure she approved, but
hadn't said so to Anthea. She was old enough to lead
her own life and learn from her own mistakes.

And Marcus didn't have to know the flat would be
empty, unless she chose to tell him.

The restaurant was expensive, with discreet lighting,
deep plush carpets and gold silk hangings on the walls.
It was small and probably exclusive. No riff-raff welcome
here, Hayley thought ironically. She recognised some
well-known faces among the other diners as they were
led to their table by the haughty head waiter, who pulled
out her seat and flicked at it with a spotless white cloth
before inviting her to sit. Feeling slightly intimidated,
Hayley sat.

'You might have told me.' She whispered the com-
plaint. 'I could have turned up in jeans and a jumper.'

'Then I'd have had to take you to my favourite caff.'

'Where *you'd* have looked totally out of place instead
of me.'

Marcus's expression was one of wry amusement. It
softened as he caught the gleam of panic in the dark
velvet depths of her eyes.

'You look very lovely,' he said softly, and covered her
hand with his own as it lay on the table. He added with
a hint of mischief that made her smile, 'And at least
twice as delicious as anything offered on the menu.'

It was said to reassure her, she knew, and she smiled
back at him gratefully.

And he'd lied, of course. The food was indescribable,
like none she'd ever tasted, although she couldn't afterwards have accurately recalled what they'd eaten. The
memory was blurred by her happiness. She simply
couldn't believe what was happening. There were women
here tonight who were probably among the most

beautiful in the world, but Marcus had eyes, it seemed, only for Hayley.

The man she could have cheerfully murdered this morning had disappeared. The man who had taken his place she could only love.

She was almost floating with happiness. Superstitiously she kept telling herself there must be some point to his invitation and soon he would tell her what it was, but he seemed intent only on giving her a wonderful time.

Hayley felt herself falling more and more in love with him as his personality unfolded before her in a way she had never imagined. He was strong and yet gentle, warm, witty and charming.

She responded with every fibre of her being, tinglingly aware of this man's powerful male sexuality. His deep, faintly husky voice thrilled her senses, making her want just to go on endlessly listening.

He'd been telling her a particularly funny anecdote from his student days and she laughed uninhibitedly, until she remembered their surroundings and lifted fingers to her mouth in sudden consternation.

'Oh! Shh! I'm sorry.'

He took the hand away and captured it between both of his, unexpectedly lifting it to his lips for a brief kiss.

'Don't be sorry. Just go on being yourself. Delightful.'

Hayley felt the burning sensation all the way down to her toes, which curled in her stylish shoes.

The question came out of the blue. 'How old are you, Hayley?'

She flushed, wondering suddenly if he found her childish.

'Twenty-three,' she said a little defensively.

He nodded. 'Do you have any family?'

'Only my mother. But I never see her now. My father died when I was fifteen. Mother got married again when I was eighteen to an Australian.'

His voice was soft. 'Did that create problems?'

Hayley shrugged. 'Not really. I missed my father, of course. We were close. But my mother is the kind of person who needs to have somebody, and Mike was nice. I liked him, and Mother was happy. But he wanted to take us both back to Australia, and I didn't want to go. I wanted to stay here and finish college. Mother spent some time trying to persuade me, and then suddenly gave up and went, just before I'd completed my course.'

'And you've been alone ever since.' He still had hold of her hand and was rubbing his thumb absently against her smooth skin, creating more than just friction heat.

She tugged it away, feeling a little irritable. 'That's the way I like it.'

He moved his head a little, as though in acceptance. 'Then you don't subscribe to your mother's feeling that everybody needs somebody.'

'Not particularly. Unless it's somebody you really want to be with. I'd rather be alone than just fill the gap.'

Those disconcerting blue eyes were full on her, searching her face until she thought she would scream.

Then he said, 'I'm thirty-five.'

'I know.' She said it too quickly, and then flushed. Now he would know she'd been peeking into his personal file.

He raised his brows. 'What else do you know?'

'Not a lot. You're thirty-five, head of a thriving company, and you've never married.' Then, outrageously, 'Why not?'

'Head of a thriving company,' he repeated. 'That's part of it, I suppose.' He shrugged. 'Or perhaps I just never got around to it.'

'Don't you want children?' The question was tentative, because his expression had closed a little.

'That's not something I've given too much thought to in the past.'

'But now?' Where was she finding the audacity? she wondered in silent amazement. Something, somehow, had shifted place. No longer boss and secretary. They were two people, interested and exploring.

'Now maybe it's time to think.' He smiled, his blue eyes deepening as they settled on her face, seeming happy with what they saw. 'Any more questions?'

Hayley lowered her gaze from his and flushed a little. He saw too much...understood too much. 'No more questions.'

She was no longer sure she would like the answers.

He'd been in a mood all day, presumably because of the picture of Felicity and her 'latest' which had appeared in the paper the day before. Had he been considering the actress for a new role as wife and mother of the children he was now beginning to think about? Did he fear he'd left the thinking too long and that now Felicity might have got tired of waiting?

She shook her head, dislodging the thoughts. Why spoil things by surmising? Whatever else, she'd had this one perfect evening to remember.

'Good,' he said, misunderstanding her nod, 'I think the next course is about due.'

The sweet arrived—a deliciously light blackcurrant cheesecake—and she gave it her full attention. She might never eat food to equal this again.

When eventually the meal was over and they were ready to leave, Hayley was torn between regret and a tingling anticipation of what might still lie ahead. The flat would be empty, and she had made up her mind that she would ask him in for coffee.

Outside, they stood on the kerb as a uniformed man hailed them a taxi. They stood close, Marcus easy and relaxed, with his arm slung lightly about her waist. Feeling happy, Hayley smiled up at him, and he bent to touch her lips lightly with his.

A light bulb flashed suddenly near by, and his head shot up with an irritable snap. Hayley heard Marcus swear, and stumbled as he released her. She saw him

moving towards a figure made hazy by the dazzle, before
a second flash blinded her. When she could eventually
focus again the uniformed man was bundling someone
away from the entrance, and Marcus had hold of her
again and was ushering her towards a taxi.

Seated beside him in the back seat, Hayley could feel
the hard tensing of his body, which seemed to burn with
the force of his anger, the heat reaching her through the
thin material of her skirt.

He was silent, staring ahead with an expressionless
intensity.

Hayley shivered with nervous reaction, and he reached
absently for her hand, squeezing her fingers gently.

'Wh-what happened?' she asked eventually. 'Who was
that man?'

'God knows!' he ground out furiously, his grip unconsciously tightening. 'Nosy parker or paparazzi. It will
come to the same thing.'

He released her hand suddenly and jerked back forcefully in his seat. He spoke almost under his breath, and
Hayley caught the words 'fool' and 'mistake'.

She sank miserably back in her seat. The evening that
had seemed so perfect had been spoiled, and there was
nothing she could do to repair matters.

The silence stretched between them, a tangible thing,
and dimly she began to realise that the brush with the
photographer wasn't just an annoyance which he would
soon shrug off. It had really upset him. Why? A man
in his prominent position? He must be used to it by now.
Having his picture in the newspapers could hardly be a
new experience.

It dawned on her then that his picture would probably
be in the morning's paper, and so would hers.

Hayley's insides curled into a tight, hard ball. Was
that why he was so furious? Because he'd been spotted
in a clandestine evening out with his secretary?

By the time the taxi drew up outside the flat Hayley was as tense and angry as Marcus.

As he got out, holding out his hand to help her, she ignored it and clambered out inelegantly, and with her eyes downcast to conceal the fury that had built up behind them.

As the taxi pulled away she looked up, her expression carefully composed, her voice wooden. 'Thank you for a lovely evening. I can't remember when I've enjoyed anything so perfect.'

It was the truth, but her tone was overhung with bitterness.

Despite everything, she still wanted him, was still silently praying he would restore the mood of earlier and ask to come in.

'Hayley,' he said, his voice gentle, despite the frown which had etched itself deeply into his brow. 'I'm sorry...'

She drew in a short audible breath and said sharply, 'Don't apologise, please. There's no need.'

'Isn't there?'

He looked at her intently for a moment, as though trying to assess her feelings, and then nodded.

'Will you be all right?' His head turned as he gazed searching about the apparently empty street.

He wasn't coming in. Hayley bit hard on her lower lip and nodded silently.

He seemed anxious to get away and, as his head descended to kiss her, she turned so that his lips met her cheek.

With an exasperated sound he caught her chin between finger and thumb, forcing her to look up at him. Seeing her stubborn expression, he sighed and released his hold.

'Goodnight, Hayley. And I really am sorry.'

Sorry! Hayley repeated the word over and over as she lay sleepless. Sorry for what? Sorry that the lovely evening had been spoiled? Or that he'd been caught out with his secretary, when he really would have preferred no one else to know about it?

The little restaurant now seemed furtive, rather than exclusive, a place where clandestine meetings were possible, almost condoned, and discovery was practically impossible. But not quite, as Marcus had just found out, to his obvious fury.

The thought made her feel cheap, soiled...the way Frank Heaton's gropings had done. But the hurt was deeper, more personal.

Because now she was in love. Deeply and hopelessly. She wished desperately that she hadn't let it happen, and tears slid silently to soak the pillow, stinging her cheek.

Well, it was too late for regrets now, she thought bitterly. Her regrets...or his.

CHAPTER EIGHT

STUDYING her face in the bathroom mirror, Hayley groaned. She looked as dreadful as she felt. Last night's tears were clearly visible in the puffy blue smudges beneath her eyes. And today, Friday, was the first of the long-distance meetings, which Marcus had briefed her as being one of the most difficult. She only hoped she was up to it.

There would be one final company to be dealt with tomorrow morning, the distance and the early start necessitating her and Marcus staying over tonight in a hotel. She hoped she would be up to that as well. It would take every ounce of her resolve to maintain the necessary cool.

Over that fabulous dinner, for a little while the barriers between them had come down and she had begun to hope. In the clear light of morning she knew she'd been chasing fool's gold.

She turned away from the mirror and went to find her weekend bag. Last night, full of Marcus's unexpected dinner invitation, she had forgotten to pack, and had had to get up extra early to repair the omission. In no mood to be selective, she threw in a couple of skirts and blouses, the first that came to hand. As an afterthought she packed her midnight-blue cocktail dress, followed by a nightdress, bathrobe and toilet bag.

That finished, she rummaged at the back of the wardrobe for something to put on now. In her present rather crotchety mood, nothing seemed to appeal.

She was just trying on a black dress made of very fine wool which clung to her curves, dipping coyly to a hint of cleavage and barely reaching to her knees, wondering if she dared wear it to a formal meeting, when Anthea came breezing in.

'Oh, that looks great on you, Hay!' She gave a mock-mournful sigh. 'It just doesn't seem right that you should have that lovely face and the fabulous figure to go with it. I think whoever was in charge of distributing these things might have thought to share them around a little more fairly.'

Hayley said drily, 'There's nothing wrong with what you were given in the way of looks. It's the scatty personality you want to work on. Where were you last night?'

Anthea stared at her. 'Where do you think?'

'I'd rather not think,' Hayley said, and waved her hand dismissively as Anthea's mouth opened indignantly. 'Don't say anything. It's not my business. I just thought I'd let you know how I feel about Lenny Barnes.'

'Well, thanks! He's no handsome hunk, it's true! But we're not all as lucky as you!' Anthea said somewhat aggressively. 'Perhaps if I were a little more cool and uppity, like you, I'd make the same kind of impact on Marcus Maury that you do.'

Hayley grimaced. 'About as much impact as a new computer. Perhaps less.'

Anthea laughed derisively. 'Oh, come on! Surely you're not going to play games with me this morning? Not after what I've just seen in the paper.'

There were two pictures, one with Marcus kissing her as they waited for the taxi, and the other showing Marcus angrily in pursuit of the photographer and Hayley in the background, her dazzled eyes looking strange and glassy and frightened.

The headline read: 'Yet Another Maury Merger'.

In a way she was relieved to find that Marcus hadn't yet arrived at the office. The phone was ringing shrilly, the noise jarring Hayley's overstretched nerves, making her abrupt.

'Marcus Maury's office.'

A woman's voice. 'Is he there?'

'I'm afraid not. I'm his secretary. May I take a message?'

'Well; well! Miss Morgan!' Felicity Braun's voice was hardly recognisable, sounding hoarse rather than huskily seductive this morning, as though she'd done some unaccustomed shouting or maybe a little crying. 'So you've finally come out of hiding.'

'I beg your pardon? I don't understand.'

'I think you do. The pictures flatter you, don't you think? Nevertheless; congratulations! First round to you.'

Hayley's heart began to thump. Felicity had obviously seen the newspaper, and it had made her fighting furious. Had Marcus seen it yet? she wondered, feeling a little sick.

'You set your trap very neatly. The prim, proper little secretary act before bringing on the vamp. You might have fooled Marcus, but not me. I had your number right from the start.'

'You may think so, Miss Braun, but you're mistaken.'

'Oh, I'm never mistaken.' A surprisingly coarse laugh echoed down the line. 'And I've never yet lost a man I've really wanted.'

Hayley's temper boiled. 'Is that the message you'd like me to pass on, Miss Braun?'

Felicity said sweetly, 'That message is for you, dearie, so don't say you haven't been warned. Tell Marcus I'm sorry I couldn't make it last night, but I'll be free this evening.'

The click of the line being cut seemed to have a triumphant sound, and Hayley slammed her receiver down with a vicious bang.

So that had been the reason for the impulsive invitation to dinner last night! Felicity had stood him up and he hadn't wanted to cancel a booking!

Hayley's insides clenched sickeningly, remembering the eagerness with which she'd accepted, the pains she'd taken with her appearance, the way she'd opened up to him about her family, when all he'd been interested in was whiling away an empty evening.

And to think she'd been on the point of asking him into the flat, with God knew what on her mind if he'd accepted. But she couldn't deny it to herself. She'd wanted him to make love to her. If it hadn't been for the photographer ruining his mood, perhaps it all might have happened the way she'd desperately wanted it to. Thank God it hadn't.

She groaned aloud and chewed fretfully at her lower lip. How was she going to face him now she knew?

He came rushing in five minutes later, as she was putting the mail folder on his desk. She turned as he came in through the door and their eyes met, hers wary, his just about the same as every other morning, she noticed in amazement.

'Overslept,' he announced, moving around behind his desk but not sitting. Without even looking at it, he slipped the post file into a drawer and locked it, pocketing the key. 'I hope you're ready to go right now. Otherwise we're late.'

'I know.' Hayley nodded. 'I'll get my jacket.'

'Don't move,' he said suddenly, and frowned.

Hayley stopped, riveted to the spot. 'What is it?'

'That dress.' His eyes swept over her, inch by inch, slowly, as though afraid he'd miss something.

Hayley squirmed under his excruciating scrutiny. 'What's the matter with it?'

'Everything,' he said flatly. 'Perhaps the disguise was the right idea after all.'

'I could change——'

'No time now,' he said abruptly. 'Just get your jacket and let's go.'

He didn't even mention the newspaper pictures. Perhaps he hadn't yet seen them.

The morning was bright and sunny as they sped along the quiet roads, and the countryside had never looked lovelier, Hayley thought, knowing it was the chemistry sparked off by the nearness of Marcus which made the whole world seem dazzling.

Angry, hurt and disillusioned as she was, she was still an easy victim to his overwhelming masculinity.

She stole surreptitious glances at him, drinking in the strong lines of his profile, which had as much impact as though she were seeing it for the first time. Her whole body tingled with awareness.

He turned and caught her glance, giving her a quirky little smile that might have meant anything.

'Questions?'

Embarrassed, she rushed into speech with the first question that sprang to mind. 'Will the merger management team be there today?'

He gave a short, dry laugh. 'If you mean young Lukes, yes, he will.'

Hayley flushed. 'I . . . I didn't mean . . .'

He shot her a brief, assessing look, missing nothing of the tell-tale heat in her cheeks.

He said almost jeeringly, 'He's of your generation and quite clever when he's paying attention to his work. You could do worse.'

'Oh, but I don't . . .' She faltered to a halt, dismayed by the barrier that had grown, with amazing speed, between them. A barrier over which she found it impossible to climb.

He said abruptly, 'You don't have to explain anything to me.'

'That's true,' she said, with a sudden flash of temper. 'And thanks. I'll bear your character assessment in mind.'

He was right. Felicity was still in his life. And if she were the smallest bit interested in Martin Lukes, then he undoubtedly could be in hers...

But she wasn't... and he wasn't...

She sat alongside him, looking miserably out of the window at a world that had suddenly lost its sparkle.

As it turned out, Martin Lukes was the first person she saw on their arrival at the meeting. He was even more impeccably dressed than usual, Hayley noted with a little start of surprise, and it was obvious he'd made a special effort. If his intention had been to create an impression, then he'd certainly made one on her, she thought with a little smile, and if Marcus wanted to divert her in the direction of Martin Lukes then she would allow herself to be diverted.

And she found that surprisingly easy as her gaze remained on the friendly young accountant. It was the first time she'd noticed how handsome he was. His broad face with its pleasantly arranged features beamed with health and vitality, and his blond hair positively gleamed in the rays of the sun thrown obliquely through the tall windows of the boardroom.

Martin's warm brown eyes returned her assessment, and as his gaze swept her from head to toe in frank admiration she was glad she hadn't changed her dress.

'Good morning.' She smiled at him.

'And good morning to you.'

He shook her hand, his hold lingering a little before releasing her fingers.

'You look positively stunning, Miss Morgan.' His voice was softly appreciative, his expression blatantly teasing. 'Does my good luck stretch to our having lunch together today?'

'I haven't brought my crystal ball.' She gave him a mock-mysterious look. 'But I shouldn't be at all surprised.'

They laughed, their amusement sounding loud in the quietening room, and she was suddenly aware of a peculiar sensation in the back of her neck, a kind of tingling awareness. She turned to find Marcus staring over at her. Their eyes met across the heads of the people gathered for the meeting, his electric-blue and icy, drawing her without words or gesture in his direction, hers clouded with confusion.

How had he done that; penetrated her consciousness when she'd been engrossed in conversation with somebody else? The power of the man was frightening, she acknowledged, with a shiver that rippled through her slim body.

The room seemed to fall hushed and silent around them as she struggled to release her gaze from his.

Martin Lukes broke the spell.

'It looks as though the great man is about to begin the business,' he said, sounding faintly ironic. 'So I'll see you later.'

'Yes.' Hayley's cheeks were still stinging from the sudden rush of colour that Marcus's imperious look had elicited.

Well, she thought in sudden rebellion, he'd virtually pointed Martin Lukes out to her as someone of interest, so why the cold annoyance?

Impulsively, and more than a little defiantly, she reached up and placed a light kiss on Martin's cheek.

'I look forward to that.'

Marcus Maury's steely gaze was still on her as she made her way across the room, but she refused to meet it and, with lowered head, took her seat beside him.

Today the meeting seemed less than absorbing and, as the time wore on towards twelve-thirty, Martin Lukes directed an anticipatory wink at her, but it was another half-hour before the morning session was brought to a close.

Marcus took her arm as she stood up to leave.

'Hayley, don't go too far. I'll be with you in a moment.'

She stood uncertainly while he held a low conversation with one of the directors of the merging company, and Martin Lukes came up to stand beside her.

'Problems?' He raised blond brows quizzically. 'Has the great man chained you to his side for lunch?'

'I don't know,' she said uneasily, wishing Martin didn't sound quite so antagonistic. 'Perhaps you'd better go on and find the canteen or something.'

Martin's mouth set stubbornly. 'Don't worry. I'll wait.'

When Marcus came back they were standing side by side in uncomfortable silence. For some reason Hayley was nervous.

Marcus paused on his way over to have a word with his own head of finance, and then came towards them.

'On second thoughts, I'll be quite a while longer,' he said, with a frown between his brows. 'No point in your hanging about here. Perhaps Lukes can find you some lunch.'

'No problem.' A wide smile had spread across Martin's broad face.'

'Good!' Marcus said, but his tight expression didn't look as though he saw any good in the situation. 'Be back in an hour.'

Martin grabbed Hayley's hand firmly. 'If time's that short, we'd better get a move on.'

Hayley, suffering from strangely mixed feelings, let herself be led off. It took her a while to notice he was heading for the car park.

'The canteen's over there.' She pointed to a single-storey building set apart.

He'd reached his car and unlocked the passenger door. 'We're not lunching in the canteen, my sweet. There's a very nice country inn not too far away, and I thought it would be nice if we dined in style. I'm celebrating.'

Hayley laughed. 'Do you think an hour is long enough for a celebration?'

He grinned. 'Probably.'

'What's the celebration?' she asked ten minutes later. They were seated at a table for two in the cottage eating area of the inn, and the waitress had just brought them home-made steak and kidney pie with vegetables. It looked delicious.

'My new job. I heard I'd got it yesterday.'

Hayley was momentarily stunned. 'You're leaving Maury's?'

'Don't look so surprised. People do, you know. Leave Maury's, I mean.'

Hayley wondered why she felt so dismayed.

'Won't your leaving cause somewhat of a disruption of the Maury take-overs?'

Martin shrugged. 'Oh; I'll see that through to a reasonable point. I'm not exactly indispensable, but I won't cause any more problems than I have to.'

Hayley sighed. 'Well, that's something anyway. I'd hate to be around Marcus for a while if you left him high and dry.'

'If I had my way you wouldn't be around Maury at all. Spoilt bastard.'

Her mouth dropped in shocked surprise. 'Martin! That's a bit strong, isn't it?'

He grinned wryly. 'Perhaps it is, but it's true. All those gorgeous women falling over themselves for him, and he treats them all like dirt.'

'That's not quite true, either.' Hayley found herself, with strangely hammering heart, defending Marcus. 'He can't help it if he's attractive. If women fall for him it's their problem. You can't expect him to give himself just because they want him.'

She stopped, struck by what she'd just said. She might
have been talking to herself, telling herself what she knew
to be the truth.

Martin groaned. 'I should be so lucky.' He shot her
a suddenly serious glance. 'You're not in love with him,
are you?'

She had her pride, didn't she? Surely it was permitted
to lie a little in the circumstances.

'No. But I like him a lot.'

'And even that's too much.'

Hayley sighed. 'You don't like Marcus, do you?' she
asked quietly.

He shrugged. 'Does any man ever like another man
that powerful? He runs my life, and I resent it.' He gave
a tight little laugh. 'Take you, for instance. He treats
you as though you were his personal property instead
of just his secretary. I've been getting some pretty strong
signals warning me off. Perhaps you don't know it, but
there's a big sign around your neck. "Don't Touch".
Who the hell does he think he is? God?'

'This pie is delicious.' Hayley changed the subject
abruptly.

Martin reached across the table and touched a tress
of her hair. 'So are you,' he said softly, and sighed. 'And
that's the pity of it.'

Hayley flushed and turned her head away. He was a
nice man. And the real pity was——

'Oh, God!' Martin groaned. 'Don't look now, but
Maury's just walked in. Are we never going to get away
from the man?'

Her head spun around quickly. He was there with a
group, and as his eyes met hers briefly and then looked
away without any further acknowledgement Hayley
paled. His face had that tight, closed look she knew so
well. He was obviously furious about something.
Perhaps, at last, he'd seen the newspapers.

*   *   *

Marcus was late back from lunch and the meeting dragged on well after the time scheduled. To everyone's obvious surprise, he seemed prepared to argue even quite minor points, and there was a communal sigh of relief when at last the business was closed.

Seated beside Marcus on the way to the hotel Liz Jarvis had booked for them, Hayley cast a glance at his hard profile and gave a silent sigh. He was obviously still very angry, and she just couldn't wait any longer to find out the reason.

'I...I suppose you saw the newspaper,' she said hesitantly.

'The newspapers?' He seemed to come out of a deep reverie. 'Oh! You mean the photographs.' He gave her a short searching look. 'Did they upset you?'

She blinked in surprise. 'No. But I thought they might have upset you.'

He shrugged. 'I've been through it all before.' His brows descended darkly. 'I'm just sorry you got dragged into the scene.'

'It wasn't your fault.'

'Nevertheless.' The word seemed to end that conversation.

He was silent for a while and then, out of the blue, he said, 'By the way, Lukes has told me he's leaving the company.'

Hayley was stunned. Why had Martin chosen to spring the news on Marcus today of all days?

'You knew, of course,' he stated, without giving her a chance to answer. 'Was the meal a thank-you for your moral support?'

'I didn't know until today,' she said woodenly. 'The meal was a celebration.'

'So that was the reason for the sexy dress.' He cast her a coolly ironic glance. 'A celebration with the boyfriend.'

Hayley stared at him, perplexed and angry. 'Martin isn't my boyfriend. And I dress to please myself.' She lifted her chin defiantly. 'I'm sure it's inconvenient for you to lose Martin at the moment, but surely he's entitled to better himself if he can.'

He grunted. 'Do you seriously think he's bettering himself? No one betters the salary I pay.'

She said doggedly, 'People's views on what's meaningful differ. Perhaps Martin looks beyond the subject of money.'

'Doubtful, I'd say.' His tone was disparaging. 'And I must say, for someone who isn't interested in Lukes, you seem to know a lot about him.'

'I didn't say I wasn't interested. I have a friendly interest.'

'So I noticed. Friendly enough for you to kiss him in public this morning.' He gave a short, hard, humourless laugh. 'But then I forgot; that's your usual style, isn't it, Miss Pushy?'

His attack surprised and dismayed her. It showed he still hadn't forgotten that foolish incident. She might have guessed he'd dig it out and use it against her at some time.

She said at last, hiding her visibly shaking hands in her lap, 'That was a long time ago, Mr Maury.' It seemed like a lifetime.

'Not that long.' His voice was softly jeering. 'You never did explain it. And you're still pretty free with your kisses.'

Hayley's mouth trembled, but she bit hard on her bottom lip to steady it.

'If it makes you happy to think that, then go ahead,' she said dully. 'I'd rather not discuss it.'

He grimaced. 'And I'm damned sure I would prefer to forget it.'

She turned on him angrily. 'Then why don't you? After all, it doesn't really concern you. I'm only your secretary. Anyone would think...'

She broke off as he shot her a hostile, enquiring look that dared her to go on.

'That you were jealous.' The words were out before she could stop them and she gave a little gasp, putting her hand to her mouth.

He looked stunned and then furious.

'I'm sorry,' she said, her voice barely audible. 'That was a silly thing to say.'

The car slowed and drew to a halt at the side of the road. Releasing the seatbelts, he caught her arms in a grip of steel.

'Is it silly?' he demanded in a voice that was strangely hoarse, and then answered his own question. 'Yes, I suppose it is. But the real stupidity is in trying to pretend that it isn't true.'

Hayley's eyes widened on his. 'I...I don't understand.'

'Don't you? I should have thought it was obvious.' He pulled her closer. 'Yes, I'm jealous. When I saw you kissing him this morning I could have hit him and wrung your lovely neck.'

His mouth came down savagely on hers, giving her no time to absorb his astounding admission. With the warm pressure of his mouth against hers, persuasive, parting her own to taste the inner sweetness, it would soon be impossible to think of anything more than the sensations his kiss was arousing.

But she tried, knowing this was madness. In fact everything that had happened between them had been madness and they would both regret this later, when the adrenalin ebbed and sanity returned. She wished she could tell him all this, but his mouth was exploring hers with a famished intensity that was sweeping her own senses away.

A strange kind of yearning began somewhere deep inside her and she shivered as he drew her even closer, his hands moving against her waist and the gentle curve of her hip. She strained towards him, her lips answering his with their own need, her body seeming to catch fire with the heat of her longing.

She heard him groan and was aware of a searing disappointment as he began to move away from her. Involuntarily she clutched at him, and he laughed softly.

'Hayley, this is an English country road and it's still broad daylight,' he murmured. 'Neither the time nor the place.'

As he moved back, Hayley's eyes held his in clouded confusion, her hands gripping the lapels of his jacket in a mute question. What was this? Some kind of game to relieve the tedium of the day?

He gave a little laugh. 'We'll talk later, Hayley. In the meantime, here's something to think about.'

Leaning forward, he pressed a light, soft kiss against her mouth. It was over in a second, but he was right. The sensation haunted her for a long time afterwards.

He started up the car again and she sat in a kind of a daze, questions chasing around in her head.

How could she have let him kiss her that way; let herself respond to him with absolutely no resistance? And what kind of jealousy had he admitted to? Probably the dog-in-the-manger type of jealousy Martin had accused him of. She was his secretary, bought and paid for, with a sign that commanded 'Don't touch'. Except himself, of course, when he was in the mood.

And where was her old resentment at the casual way he'd claimed her? Why hadn't she fought him with all the fury and disdain such chauvinism should have aroused? The answer to that lay in her feelings for him, which led her, at some deep unconscious level, to hope ... knowing such hope was an act of self-deceit.

Rationally she knew that to him his lovemaking was a game, a shameful game of 'When the cat's away...' And if she had any pride...any common sense, she would make sure she kept a cool head as far as he was concerned.

But at the moment she was far from cool.

The thought of staying overnight with him in a hotel loomed over her, but despite everything she was aware of a deep, tantalising anticipation. How could her mind and feelings be split this way? He was dangerous, she acknowledged, to her peace of mind and her pride, but he drew her like a chasm to its edge. Would she be able to follow without jumping off to her own destruction?

She was disturbed by the look the receptionist gave them as they signed the register. Marcus was looking handsome, distinguished, amazingly fresh still in his expensive business suit and crisp white shirt. And she stood alongside in her sexy dress, with her hair a little wild and probably her lipstick smudged. When Marcus politely passed her the register for her signature, she was glad her name was Morgan and not Smith.

She was even more disturbed to discover, as they were escorted to the first floor, that they had been given adjoining rooms.

'I've booked dinner for eight,' Marcus said curtly once the girl, with a last curious glance, had left them. 'I'll give your door a knock around then.'

He seemed absorbed in his own thoughts, turning to enter his room with only a brief glance in her direction.

Hayley's spirits sank. She herself had predicted that when he'd cooled off he would regret the searing moments of passion in the car, but it still hurt to be proved right. When are you going to regain your sanity, girl? she admonished herself, knowing she should be feeling gladness, instead of this odd deflation. The more distance he kept between them, the less likely she would be to make a fool of herself.

She consoled herself with a leisurely bath and then set about choosing something to wear. The skirts and blouses were formal office wear, she realised, silently cursing her contrary mood of the morning. The only possible choice was the midnight-blue cocktail dress that she'd worn to the première. Its thin straps seemed hardly capable of holding it up and, observing the plunge of the neckline, she was almost tempted to take it off and wear a skirt and blouse after all.

But the dress was a real favourite of hers. It made her feel good, boosted her confidence, and goodness knew it could do with a little boosting tonight.

She smoothed the silky fabric over her trim hips and regarded her reflection critically, but she could find no fault. It turned her light tan to honey-gold and enhanced her slim waist and full rounded bosom. Her shapely legs looked slim and elegant in matching strappy sandals.

Her hair, loosed from its restraining coil, sprang vibrantly from the brush and rioted in a cloud of rich dark brown curls. A little light eye make-up and some lipstick added a glow, and she cast a last satisfied glance in the mirror just as his knock sounded on the door.

His brows rose in silent appreciation as she stood framed in the doorway, and she felt her colour rise at the warm glint in his blue eyes, which sent shivers of response down her spine.

She managed a calm smile, stepping out into the corridor and locking the door behind her. 'I hope there's something good on the menu. I'm starving.'

'It would have to be very good to beat what I'm looking at.'

Hayley stifled a sigh. She wished he wouldn't say things like that. It confused her. One minute he was furious with her and the next full of admiration.

'More of those swings and roundabouts you warned me about?' she queried, looking him straight in the eye, hoping she'd find some clue to guide her through the evening.

He laughed, his eyes crinkling with amusement. 'I should have warned myself,' he said.

And what was she to make of that?

Dinner was served in the large dining-room at the rear of the hotel, overlooking a beautiful informal garden and an ornamental lake. There were lights hung in the trees, which would no doubt be lit at dusk to add to the charmed atmosphere.

'You look delightful, Hayley,' Marcus said softly, the words vibrating along her nerves like music on a finely tuned instrument. 'A fresh surprise every time I look at you.'

'Thank you,' Hayley murmured, glad of the interruption as the waiter served their first course.

'This is spinach?' she said, her brows rising.

There was a neat little parcel of pastry on her plate, its four corners pointing into the middle, a creamy white sauce oozing from the folds.

She cut into it and took a mouthful. 'Mmm. Wonderful!'

Marcus laughed. 'What's wonderful is the way you enjoy things. It almost makes it worth what it probably cost.'

The rest of the meal lived up to the start, the wines changing with the courses. She drank only a little of each, but felt decidedly heady by the time coffee was served. The rich, strong brew, sipped slowly because it was hot, took the headiness away and left the happiness.

She looked around the quietly luxurious room and said drily, 'For a stopover hotel, Liz certainly broke the bank with this one. I'm sure she could have found a cheaper one.'

'She did,' he said, his mouth curving at one corner. 'I changed reservations.'

Hayley's mouth dropped open. 'But why?'

'Because I knew you'd like it.' He reached across the table and took her hand, his thumb brushing lightly against the palm, creating eddies of excitement. 'And because this one is more romantic.'

His eyes were a softer captivating blue, luring her into their smouldering depths. Somewhere a little warning bell was ringing.

She didn't smile. 'Are you sure you don't mean seductive?'

He sighed and took his hand away. 'I mean exactly what I say. When are you going to start listening?'

The wine had loosened her tongue after all. She said, 'Perhaps when I know I can trust you.'

He frowned. 'Do you have reason to think you can't?'

She shrugged, feeling a sudden spurt of anger, the rising of a fear that she had thought long-buried.

'Only in the way that I've learned not to trust any man. I used to work for a man who thought that just because he paid my salary he was entitled to take whatever liberties...'

She gave a sudden convulsive shudder. Why on earth should she have begun to think of Frank Heaton now?

His mouth was grim line. 'And what's been happening between us was...taking liberties?'

She seemed unable to stop. 'Perhaps. Your approach is more subtle, of course, but what you want is the same in the end.' She went on bitterly, 'Unfortunately for my ex-boss his looks and technique are against him, but maybe his approach is the more honest. At least there was no mistaking what he was after.'

Marcus sat back, releasing his hold on her hand, studying her from under the heavy brown lashes. 'And you think I'm after the same?'

Hayley's cold glance challenged him. 'Well, aren't you?'

He gave a short, unamused laugh. 'If you mean do I want to take you to bed and make love to you, the answer is yes. But I thought...I believed...it was what you wanted too.'

Hayley's eyes flew wide in astonishment. She hadn't expected him to admit it quite so blatantly. Neither had she thought she'd been that transparent.

'Was I wrong?'

Remembering them together in the car, the way her body had burned as he'd held her in his arms, knowing he'd felt her response, it was difficult to deny it.

'At the time...no. But the difference between you and me is that I'm free to make that kind of choice.'

His brows rose. 'And what's that supposed to mean?'

Hayley met the piercing blue gaze with a painfully thudding heart. 'Oh, come on, Marcus! Don't you know?'

It was then she remembered that she hadn't passed on Felicity's message that she was free this evening, but somehow it didn't seem to matter. Marcus hadn't been anyway. She gave a funny little giggle.

He made an impatient sound. 'Drink up your coffee. We'll finish this discussion in a more appropriate setting.'

Hayley did as he said, with a feeling of having stepped across some invisible line, and his expression told her he would allow her no avenue of retreat.

Outside in the warm night he took her arm and led her into the sheltered garden. The night was warm and scented, the sky hung with a myriad stars, but Hayley found she was shivering. She was nervous and her heart had begun to hammer quite painfully against her ribs.

She stole a glance at Marcus and saw, to her surprise and relief, that he was no longer angry.

'What you've told me makes sense of a lot of things,' he said, taking her hand and rubbing the cold fingers between his. 'Do you want to talk about it?'

'No, I don't want to talk about it, or think about it ever again.' She was shivering uncontrollably now.

He put his arm about her shoulder. 'If you'd like to go to your room...'

'No! I want to be with you.' It was a cry of anguish, and his arm tightened about her. She turned her head in against his shoulder. 'Oh, Marcus! I'm so confused. I don't know what to think any more.'

'Then don't think; just look at me.'

He raised her chin with a gentle finger so that their eyes met. All the confusion, all the pain seemed to melt away in the warm blue depths of his gaze.

'What do you see?' he asked, so softly that it was hardly a sound.

Hayley shook her head, afraid to say that in his eyes shone everything she'd ever dreamed of. Because this was a dream and soon she'd wake up.

'Do you want me as much as I want you?' he asked.

Her need was so huge, so painful. 'How much is that?'

Marcus drew her into his arms kissing her gently, tenderly, drawing a hesitant response that grew more positive as he stroked her face, her hair, her slender throat. Softly, sensuously, his mouth caressed hers, his tongue outlining her lips, thrusting gently until she met him with her own.

Somewhere deep inside her a fire had ignited, its flames licking upwards, consuming her senses. Her arms reached out to hold him, moving urgently against his strong neck, the broad, hard shoulders.

He pulled her closer, kissing her deeply, almost hungrily, his hands moving urgently against her back and down, moulding her against him, the hardness of him pressing against her thigh.

How could this happen so quickly? she asked herself in some inner recess of her mind. Why was the effect so instantaneous for them both?

As the kiss went on the magic of his mouth claimed her, firing a passion she had never before experienced.

As her taut body softened, pressing against him of its own volition, she heard a small growl deep in his throat.

Lifting his head, he looked into the soft velvet-brown eyes, glistening with excitement, and said softly, 'You've answered my question. Now I'll answer yours.'

He pushed her away and took her hand, leading her back towards the hotel and up the stairway. At the door of her room he held out his hand for the key.

Tremblingly she fumbled in her bag and then held it out to him, a stunned expression on her face. Things were happening so fast that there was no time for pondering upon her own weakness.

The door was at last open and he was drawing her inside, taking the bag from her to drop it on the floor before taking her once again into his arms.

It felt like coming home, and she wound her arms about his neck, all pretence fading as his lips moved persuasively on hers. As she pressed herself hard against him, yearning for his deeper embrace, he lifted her up and carried her effortlessly towards the bed, where he stood her again on her feet. With his lips still on hers, he slid the zip of her dress down, brushing the light material from her shoulders, slipping the belt from her waist to allow the garment to fall with a soft sighing sound about her feet. She gasped as his deft fingers unhooked her bra to reveal the hard, aroused swell of her breasts, and shuddered as his warm hand moulded her tingling flesh.

As his mouth lifted from hers and traced a path of fiery kisses down the arch of her throat she made a small cry of protest.

'Marcus.' She spoke his name in a voice husky with passion and a hint of fear.

'Hush, my love.'

Gently he pushed her back on to the bed, swiftly removing her panties, that wisp of lace, the last barrier. And then he was shrugging out of his own clothes to lie naked beside her, where the heat of him, the clean male scent of his skin, had her senses spinning dizzily. Her fingers, seemingly of their own volition, reached up to twine in his thick hair, drawing his head to hers.

As his arms reclaimed her, Hayley surrendered her lips to his, her own demands matching his, her sighs and moans a symphony with his deeper tones.

Sucked down into the vortex of pure feeling Hayley wanted nothing more than for this ecstasy to go on and on.

With his lips and hands exploring every silky inch of her, she moved restlessly, a mounting tide of sensation demanding more, and still more, arching her towards the hardness of him, beseeching the fulfilment of union.

Slowly, relentlessly, he drove her on as wave after wave of inexplicable pleasure washed over her, until at the peak of her frustration she cried out and he moved to enter her, bringing them both to the thrusting rhythmic climax her body craved.

She slept in his arms, and when she awoke he was out of bed, standing in the window, gazing out at the moonlit night, the lithe muscularity of his body forming a silhouette that had her heart jumping once more to an erratic beat.

She must have made a sound, because he turned and came towards her, powerful and mysterious in the dim light of the moon.

Without a word, he got into bed and put his arms about her, drawing her into the hollow of his shoulder and pressing his lips against her smooth forehead.

'Marcus,' she murmured softly, 'why did we let this happen?'

He made a low sound of exasperation. 'Because it was pointless to go on pretending it wasn't inevitable.' He smoothed her cheek with a gentle hand. 'I've wanted you right from the first. It just wasn't...convenient...to admit it.'

Hayley frowned and moved back from him a little. 'That's a funny word to use. "Convenient".'

He grimaced. 'It's exactly the right word. Do you think I was pleased to have my whole tidy world turned upside-down by a chit of a girl who had no respect for my years or my consequence?'

She giggled and touched his cheek, tracing the lines beside his mouth with a soft finger. 'You make yourself sound like a pompous old man. Which is nonsense.'

'It's what I might have become, given time and enough vacuous women.'

'You've certainly had plenty of those,' Hayley said with a sharp, unexpected surge of annoyance. 'And the choice was yours, wasn't it?'

He sighed. 'Yes and no. Sometimes choices are made as a result of the past. But, like you, I don't want to think of the past right now. The present is all I need...all I want.'

He nibbled at her ear, creating the most exquisite sensations in places of which she had been only dimly aware, but Hayley clung grimly to her sense of grievance. He hadn't mentioned the future.

'The past can't be held responsible forever,' she argued hotly. 'In my opinion, a man gets the woman he deserves.'

He met her anger with a soft laugh and, in the dimness, lights danced in the muted blue of his eyes.

His long, lean fingers gently cupped her cheek.

'I hope you're right. Though I don't know what I've done to deserve you.'

Hayley narrowed her eyes on his handsome face, finding there an unexpected intensity.

She said, with elation, 'Not much...until now.' And watched his eyes turn smoky.

'Of what are you complaining?'

His grammar was perfect, she thought inconsequentially. As was everything else about him.

In a gesture that surprised them both by its daring, she trailed a hand across his tautly muscled stomach, letting her fingers linger in the dark curling hairs. She was surprised and excited by his jerk of response.

He grasped her wrist as she was about to repeat the movement.

'Behave!' He kissed her nose.

She challenged him with a grin. 'Why should I? It's time I had my way for a change.'

He took her chin in his strong, lean hand, looking her steadily in the eyes, and in a silver shaft of moonlight the depths of his seemed fathomless. 'Do you imagine it hasn't been your way all along the line?'

Her mouth dropped in real astonishment. 'What do you mean by that?'

He groaned in exasperation. 'I mean that if I'd had my way I would have had you in my arms long before now.'

Her body tensed and grew cool. She said tightly, 'I bet. If it had been convenient.'

He tutted. 'Hear me out before you get touchy.' His mouth brushed hers sweetly, coaxing it back to softness.

'In a way you're right. My future was clear ahead of me and you were an unlooked-for complication.' He sighed deeply. 'But we both know the magic was there, practically from the start.' His certainty brooked no argument. 'Being a fatalist, I accepted it was the way it was. I wanted you and was almost certain you wanted me, but I felt I had to go slow, take my time, hope that, if I was patient enough, that prickly barrier you'd erected between us would eventually fall.'

Hayley was silent, stunned by the knowledge that he'd been aware all the time of what she'd been trying to hide from him.

He brushed the hair tenderly away from her face, a gesture that had her insides somersaulting wildly.

'I didn't know why you kept shutting yourself off from me, but I was content to wait for you to come to me.' His face darkened, and Hayley felt the slight stiffening of his body. 'That is, until young Lukes turned up on the scene. Then I knew I had to make a move.'

Hayley's heart was as light as air. 'You didn't *have* to. Not on Martin's account, anyway.' She snuggled close to him. 'But I'm glad you did.'

The strange inner flame was kindling again, and she didn't really care about the whys and wherefores any more. Only this moment seemed of any real importance. Wrapping her arms about him, she reached for his lips, and heard him gasp as she moulded her soft body enticingly against him.

'My God; Hayley! You learn fast.'

'I have a good tutor,' she murmured huskily. 'Teach me some more.'

CHAPTER NINE

THE meeting the following morning was taking place in a small conference centre on the edge of a small town, the small town where Hayley had grown up, but that all seemed a long time ago, part of another life almost.

Seated at the long, shining table with Marcus and the merger management team, waiting for the directors of the last merging company to arrive. Hayley's insides burned with impatience. And, from the surreptitious glances she kept shooting at Marcus, she could see he too was feeling the strain. The realisation brought her a powerful thrill, and when he unexpectedly squeezed her hand beneath the table it was as much as she could do to keep from trembling.

Was it her imagination, she wondered, or were people looking meaningfully in their direction? There were times when every eye seemed to be focused upon them, but it was probably all in her head. Still reeling from Marcus's early morning lovemaking, Hayley felt sure her inner glow must be obvious to everyone.

The Press were at this final meeting and a tall, tough-looking reporter elbowed his way towards Marcus with a notebook in his hand and a determined gleam in his light grey eyes.

Hayley moved away as he engaged Marcus in conversation about his plans for the future of the various companies Maury's was acquiring, trying to hide her impatience as the interview became prolonged.

The door at the far end of the room opened and two men entered. Marcus acknowledged their presence with a nod and turned to dismiss the reporter with a brief handshake.

'If you'll excuse me, I think the meeting can now begin.' He cast a glance across at Hayley. 'Miss Morgan, if you wouldn't mind...'

He turned and walked away, leaving her to follow.

She watched the lithe movements of his body and thought achingly of the time they'd spent alone, wondering if was all the time there would ever be. After today, would their relationship be back to 'business as usual'?

But in the next moment even that painful thought was swiftly erased from her mind. As she took her place beside Marcus, she had a shock that drove the air from her lungs and paralysed her body. Seated at the far end of the table was Mr Heaton Senior, with a widely grinning Frank alongside him.

How she managed to go on sitting there, she would never know. Her every instinct was to flee and hide, as she had that fateful day on the train. Only now there was nowhere to run.

Forcing herself to look straight ahead, she met Frank's gloating gaze, and shook with revulsion. Automatically her hand reached beneath the table for Marcus, her fingers gripping him just above the knee.

He gave a faint start and looked in her direction, meeting her hunted expression with a frown. His hand covered hers reassuringly and he leaned towards her.

He said in a low voice, 'What is it? You look as though you've seen a ghost.'

'I...I have,' Hayley whispered, her grip tightening on the firm muscles of his thigh, feeling his strength flowing into her. 'But I'll be all right in a moment.'

He followed her gaze, and Hayley saw Frank's eyes flicker and shift away. She gave a deep sigh of relief and turned her attention to the paperwork in front of her. How on earth had she missed the fact that Heaton's was one of the potential mergers? Then she saw the date at the head of the report, and realised this was the one that had been so long delayed.

It was typical of the way things had been with Heaton's under Frank's management, and the meeting too held the same hint of chaos. By the time they broke for coffee, Marcus looked thunderous.

Hayley escaped to the ladies' room for a breather and to survey the result of her shock. The face that stared out at her from the mirror looked pale and hunted. The bruise on her chin still showed faintly blue and yellow, more noticeable against her pallor, and she retouched it with a little make-up, then brushed and re-coiled her hair.

Feeling a little better, she stepped out into the corridor and then halted in dismay.

'Well, well! If it isn't Hayley Morgan!'

Hayley's heart lurched painfully as Frank's oily voice spoke in her ear. There was no men's room on this corridor, so it was obvious that he'd deliberately followed her.

'By all that's wonderful.'

Hayley faced the one man in all the world she hated, wondering what malicious kind of fate, piling agony on agony, had brought her old tormentor out from under his stone.

He grinned at her, and his breath, unpleasantly aromatic, wafted against her cheek. 'I was hoping we'd meet up again sooner or later.'

Hayley glared. 'And here have I been praying we never would.'

He grinned with taunting delight. 'But what an honour! To be mentioned in your prayers!'

He gripped her arm painfully tight.

'You would think so,' she said scorchingly, trying to pull free, but the more she pulled, the tighter he held her.

Looking into the leering black eyes, Hayley felt the old revulsion and, for a moment, the old helplessness. But swiftly on its heels came the realisation that she had no longer to suffer the insufferable.

'Take your hands off me, Frank Heaton,' she hissed through furiously clenched teeth. 'Now! This instant!'

'Or else what? Will you scream? I don't think so. Not here.' He laughed chillingly. 'And you should know I'm not the type to be put off by a little show of temper. In fact it excites me.' He moved closer. 'Kiss me or hit me, Hayley. You always did like to play the tease.'

There were voices, people talking and laughing. If only Marcus would come, she thought desperately, but no one appeared in the corridor.

But now fury overrode her fear. It had mounted to white heat, enough to disregard everything but her most pressing need for escape from Frank's despised attentions. As his head lowered towards her, his moist lips pursed to kiss her, restraint snapped.

She kicked him, her foot drawing back and then moving forcefully forward to connect the sharp, slim heel of her shoe with his bony shin.

With a yell of agonised surprise Frank released his hold on her and staggered back.

After a moment's stunned hesitation Hayley began to run. A quick glance over her shoulder showed Frank still clutching his injured shin, his round, florid face contorted with agony. A shaky little giggle burst from her lips.

Marcus was just coming out of the conference room as she rushed around the corner.

'I've been looking for you.'

Hayley came to a halt and clutched at his arm, panting and visibly shaken.

He stared at her, a dark frown lowering his handsome face. 'What on earth's the matter? Are you ill?'

Hayley shook her head and took a deep breath to steady her nerves. The last thing she wanted now was for Marcus to know what had happened. It could only add to the chaos of the morning.

'I was hurrying,' she said. 'I thought you might be wondering where I was.'

'You were right.' He took her elbow. 'Come on! Let's get away from here and have some lunch.'

At that moment Frank came hobbling around the corner, his florid face livid, and Marcus shot him a curious look.

To Hayley's relief, he limped by without so much as a glance in her direction, and she tugged at Marcus's arm to claim his attention.

'I think that's a marvellous idea. I'm starving. Let's go.'

Later, seated at a table for two in a country pub, Marcus sat back and looked at her, his gaze searching and intent.

'Are you going to tell me what really happened earlier, or is it another of your undiscussible topics?'

Hayley sat opposite him, feeling the colour recede, while she struggled with the formation of her reply.

'Was Heaton a former boyfriend?' he insisted impatiently. 'Have you had a lovers' quarrel?'

'Ugh! Certainly not! The very idea is revolting!'

Seeing his startled expression, she laughed. 'Sorry. Heaton Junior always has that effect on me.'

He sighed a little irritably. 'Do you want to tell me about it?'

'Not really.' Resignedly she said, 'But I suppose I should, since you saved me from his clutches once before. I used to work for his father, Heaton Senior, until his son Frank came on the scene and began his sexual harassment. I liked my job and Mr Heaton, so I did my best to ignore it, but in the end it got too much, so I left.' She grimaced. 'It was my bad luck to find he was on the train that day I met you. It was Frank I was trying to evade when I...when I...'

She felt the colour surging back into her cheeks. Only now could she feel the full embarrassment of what she'd done.

'When you kissed me,' he said, adding teasingly, 'Miss Pushy wouldn't have hesitated to say it.'

Hayley smiled faintly. 'I suppose not. But then I've never really been Miss Pushy. She was just me in an emergency.'

He leaned across the table and kissed her mouth lightly.

'Then your emergency was my good luck.'

She looked into his strong, clever face and thought how much she loved him, wishing that...

'Why didn't you tell me this before, you foolish girl?'

She shrugged, taking her gaze from his. 'I suppose I was ashamed. That kind of dirt has a tendency to stick. Frank's father didn't believe me. In fact he practically accused me of leading Junior on.'

He made a grim sound, and she rushed on.

'I couldn't be sure you'd believe me either, especially after that silly incident on the train. Let's face it, you didn't seem to have the highest opinion of me at the time.'

She looked up at him then, and he nodded.

'Point taken. But I still think you might have had more faith in me.'

Hayley said indignantly, 'After *your* behaviour on the train I didn't exactly have the highest opinion of you either.'

He shot her a frowning sideways glance, but there was a hint of laughter in the vivid blue eyes.

'Young lady, reasons apart, you got everything you deserved.'

'That's only your opinion,' she argued, hiding a grin. 'And it's just about what I'd expect from a male chauvinist like you.'

But his expression was serious again, and he reached across the table for her hand, squeezing it almost absently.

'I wondered why you jumped like a scalded cat every time I came near you.' He shook his head reprovingly. 'Friend Frank is unpleasant, but I wouldn't have thought his attentions would make you that wary of all men.'

'It went on for a long time. Almost a year. And it had a profound effect on me.'

He grunted disbelievingly. 'Why did you put up with it for so long before leaving?'

She shrugged. 'Misguided notions of loyalty to my old boss, I suppose. Before Junior came along we had a very happy working relationship.'

He looked grim. 'Loyalty stretched to ridiculous lengths, don't you think?'

She nodded. 'Yes. I know that now. And after today...' She recalled unwillingly the moist red lips which had been about to fasten on hers, and a shudder travelled the length of her slim body.

He frowned darkly. 'What happened? Did he...?'

'No. He didn't get a chance. I kicked him. Very hard.' She smiled ruefully. 'With a bit of luck he'll need hospital treatment.'

'He'll definitely need hospital treatment if he comes near you again.' Hayley had never seen Marcus look so belligerent. His expression both excited and frightened her.

'He won't,' she said hurriedly. 'I have a feeling this time he's learned his lesson.'

Marcus gave a short hard laugh. 'Let's hope so, for his sake.'

Hayley shuddered. 'Do you mind if we don't talk about it any more?'

'OK. We'll leave it for now,' he agreed, although the frown hadn't entirely disappeared. 'Let's see if we can get something to eat.'

The waitress came and they ordered the lemon sole, which was fresh and delicious, and gradually they both relaxed.

As coffee was served, he sat back and rubbed his forehead with lean fingers.

'I'm not sorry this is the last of these damned merger meetings.'

She looked at him in surprise. 'I know this morning was a mess, but up until then you seemed to be full of enthusiasm—looking forward to the challenge.'

He laughed. 'No fooling you, is there, Hayley? You're right, of course.' His lean face sobered. 'This is something that's been a long time coming. It's what my grandfather always wanted. Expansion. Unfortunately he had to wait for me to grow up before he could get any help with it, and by then it was too late . . . for him.'

It was the first time he'd allowed her a glimpse into his personal life. It made her feel good, as though they'd taken a step forward.

'Were there only the two of you? He had no son?'

'One. My father,' he said brusquely. 'But he wasn't interested in the business.' He took a sip of his coffee before going on. 'He and my mother were archaeologists who found it difficult to stay in one place for too long.' He gave a short, humourless laugh. 'Sometimes when I approached my father he would look at me with complete surprise, as though I were something he'd dug up once and forgotten about.'

Hayley bit her lip, stifling her natural sympathy. He wouldn't appreciate it, she knew.

'And your mother?'

He shrugged. 'They were two of a kind. Completely wrapped up in each other and the work they were doing. I'm sure that until I was old enough to take an interest

I was just another piece of baggage to be loaded on to a camel, or a mule, or whatever, depending on where they were at the time.'

She said, a little wistfully, 'It must have been exciting at times, though. Moving about ... seeing so much of the world.'

'Yes. Uncovering the past has a certain fascination,' he admitted ruefully. 'But I could never share their obsession.' His blue eyes danced a little. 'I had an education that must be pretty unique, I suppose. Until my grandfather put a stop to it and insisted I come back to England to get a "decent schooling".'

'And were you happy about that?'

'Very happy.' He laughed, a deep, rich sound that had her insides churning in response.

'It was then I realised my grandfather's engineering genes were stronger than the combined archaeological ones of my parents.'

His expression, fired with enthusiasm, enhanced his good looks, and she longed to reach over and touch him, but tucked her hands firmly into her lap, away from temptation. Locked into his own, rather exotic past, he seemed suddenly remote ... a stranger once again. She hardly dared go on.

'Your parents ...' she said hesitantly. 'Are they still alive?'

He nodded. 'Still happily digging away ... hardly knowing what year it is.'

'And your grandfather?'

His expression sobered. 'He died five years ago, on my thirtieth birthday.' He smiled a little wistfully. 'But he died happy, knowing someone of his own was following in his footsteps.'

He sighed and then seemed to shake himself out of his reverie.

'Sorry, but I'll have to leave you for a little while. I have a few phone calls that won't wait. I'll be as quick as I can.'

Hayley sat and thought about what he'd just revealed to her of his inner self. His drives, his motivation, always so strong, were not entirely for himself. Although he might not know it, he had more in common with his parents than he knew. He had his own obsession. Intertwined with his success, his future progress, would always be his great love for his grandfather. With a flash of insight she wondered, a little sadly, if it would preclude his ever really loving someone else.

After a while, feeling restless, Hayley made her way towards the ladies' room. Out in the foyer, she collided with a young man coming in, and stood back in surprise as she recognised him.

'Martin! What on earth are you doing here?'

Martin grinned. 'I'm here for an advance meeting with my new boss. I've been doing some emergency calculations on the company's finances. A bit borderline at the moment, but I've thought of one or two ways we might save the sinking ship.'

Hayley grinned. 'If anyone can do it, you can.' She laid a hand on his arm. 'Well, good luck.'

'Thanks. Ah! They're here already.' He was looking past her into the bar. 'Can I get you a drink before I join them?'

'Oh, no!' she said hastily. 'I'm here with—er—Marcus.'

He said drily, 'I should have guessed.' He grinned. 'But I wish you'd just let me introduce you. They'd be impressed.'

Hayley shook her head, but couldn't resist a little peek out of interest.

'Oh, my God!' There was a sick, lurching sensation in her stomach as she recognised the two men seated at one of the tables. 'The Heatons! Is that the firm you're thinking of working for?'

The colour drained from her face, and she stared up at Martin in horror.

He nodded. 'Do you know them?'

'Too well,' she said flatly. 'But don't you know? The company's a mess. They're thinking of merging with Maury's. You'll be working for Marcus again if they do.'

'That's just it.' Martin's smile showed satisfaction. 'They've almost decided not to merge, and on the basis of my figures they probably won't. Apparently it's always been a family concern and they're going to carry on trying to make a go of it, with me as chief accountant.'

Hayley laughed hollowly. 'Frank's idea, I bet. He couldn't make a go of taking the skin off a rice pudding.'

Martin looked a little dazed.

'Well, hello again, Hayley. I thought it was you.'

She'd been too involved in arguing her point to notice Junior's approach.

She shuddered visibly and said, 'Hello and goodbye.'

To Martin she said, 'Good luck. I think you might need it.'

'Oh, don't rush off. Father is so looking forward to seeing you again.'

Frank was holding her arm, drawing her across to the table where his father was sitting, looking pale but composed.

The old man gave her a hesitant smile. 'Hayley, my dear. How nice to see you again. I had no idea you knew Mr Lukes.'

Hayley nodded. 'We work together. At the Maury Corporation.'

Faint colour stained his cheeks. 'Ah! Then you'll know about the proposed merger.'

'Yes. I was there at the meeting this morning,' she said, surprised he hadn't recognised her as Frank obviously had. 'I'm Mr Maury's secretary. Does he know you're not going through with the merger?'

He shook his head. 'Not yet. Things weren't quite finalised this morning. But I hope to decide one way or another by the end of our little discussion with Mr Lukes.' He turned to Martin. 'What do you think? Can we save the company?'

Martin shrugged. 'I think it's possible. I've listed the procedures that I think would work. But they're pretty stringent.'

Mr Heaton smiled and let out an audible sigh. 'I'm so happy. I didn't really want to let the old firm go.'

Already Frank seemed bored with the subject. He was toying with his glass, his black eyes going from Martin to Hayley and back with a look of malicious amusement.

'And are *you* going to be happy to let Hayley go?' he cut in. 'Not working together, you'll miss a lot of opportunities.' He gave Martin his oily smile. 'Does she still like it the way she used to like it?'

His hand touched Hayley's shoulder and trailed across her breast. She stiffened with revulsion and brushed him away.

'What do you mean?' Martin's face had stilled.

Frank's smile widened. 'She used to like it a lot.' He winked. 'Get my meaning?'

'Quite frankly, no.'

'Oh, come on!' His black eyes raked Hayley's face. 'I see she still has her little weakness for a bit of rough stuff.' He leaned across to touch Hayley's chin. 'Is this your doing? Nice one, Martin! Nice one!'

At the touch of his hand against her skin, Hayley's control snapped.

'Take your filthy hand off me, Frank Heaton, or so help me——'

'You'll smack me like you used to?' Frank jeered. 'Yes, please. Though that kick you gave me earlier stung a bit.'

'I might have guessed your skin was too thick for any real damage,' Hayley said bitterly. 'I wish I'd kicked harder.'

Frank laughed. 'Feeling vicious, eh? Should be interesting! Perhaps I could oblige you later, if my friend here doesn't mind.'

Martin's hand shot out and grasped his shirt front. 'One more word from your foul mouth *friend*, and you'll regret it.'

'OK, OK!' Frank tugged himself free and lifted a podgy hand. People were beginning to stare, and old Mr Heaton's skin had turned a sallow yellow.

'You'll have to forgive my son,' he mumbled, with a catch in his voice. 'Unfortunately his mother spoiled him.'

Martin said belligerently, 'At the moment I would be quite happy to spoil his looks. What he has of them.' He took Hayley's arm. 'I'm really sorry I let you in for this, Miss Morgan.'

'Miss Morgan,' Frank mimicked jeeringly. 'How intimately formal. Or are you formally intimate? My pet name for her was Miss Morgasm.'

At the sound of the degrading nickname with which he'd used to taunt her, Hayley's hands flew to her ears.

'You are the most ... disgusting ...'

'I agree,' Martin gritted furiously. 'And it's time someone did something about it.'

He raised his fist, but was caught off guard as a steely hand grasped his wrist.

'If anyone is going to do anything about it, Lukes, it will be me.'

Martin's angry brown eyes challenged Marcus's icy blue ones for long seconds before finally giving way.

'Frank Heaton.' Marcus said the name as though it made a bad taste in his mouth. 'I've been hearing some pretty unsavoury things about your character,'

Frank, who had been almost cringing, faced with two angry burly men, found courage from somewhere to make a challenge.

'From Hayley Morgan?' he said, thrusting his jeering face at Marcus. 'Well, if she's your secretary you should know better than to believe her sly little lies.' He laughed unpleasantly. 'In fact I'm willing to bet there's not much else about her you don't know...intimately.'

Hayley gasped as Marcus's hard fist connected suddenly with Frank's out-thrust jaw.

With a cry of anguished humiliation she turned away and made for the exit, hearing only faintly the thud of Frank's flabby body hitting the floor.

Outside, she found herself in the midst of a group of people who'd just got off a coach, looking startled at the sound of the internal fracas.

Pushing blindly through, she walked quickly away, out of sight and sound of the bloody battle she was sure would ensue.

Marcus came and found her some time later. She'd been leaning against his car, trying to stem the flow of her tears, and as he suddenly appeared she clung to him.

'Oh, Marcus! I'm so sorry you got dragged into that.'

He said gruffly, 'It wasn't your fault. I lost my temper. Not that I'm sorry. The oily little rat had it coming.'

She burst into fresh tears and he held her for a while, his hand absently stroking her silky hair while his shirt got wet and she listened to the angry thunder of his heartbeat.

A flash bulb went off—a man among a group of tourists—and Marcus swore and waved him away.

'This is a fine bloody place to have a case of hysterics,' he said irritably.

Hayley sniffed. 'I'm not having hysterics. But if I were, I think I'd be entitled to them.'

She straightened, shocked by how deeply within his arms she'd been enwrapped. There was a sea of interested faces about them.

'Oh, my God!'

'Come on.' He shook her away from him. 'Let's get back to close that meeting. The business with Heaton's is thankfully terminated.'

'They've definitely decided not to go ahead with the merger?'

He grimaced. 'If they haven't, I have.' He opened the passenger door and pushed her in a little irritably and then came around the bonnet to get in beside her.

Hayley was glad for herself, but wondered how Martin would fare with the Heatons. No doubt he would survive, one way or another. If only he hadn't been so hasty in giving in his notice.

She looked across at Marcus and sighed, and he squeezed her knee.

'One good thing, anyway,' he said with the crooked smile she loved so much. 'It means we've got a free afternoon together.' He touched a finger against her cheek and said in a low, slightly husky voice, 'The night too, if we stay on at the hotel.'

After only a slight hesitation Hayley said, 'Then let's stay on.'

CHAPTER TEN

THEY spent the afternoon rowing on the river. Hayley lounged back, letting Marcus do the work. He'd rolled up his shirt-sleeves, revealing strong, tanned forearms liberally dusted with fine brown hairs, and through lazily narrowed lids she watched the play of his muscles, revelling in the memory of those same muscular arms holding her willing prisoner to his love.

Marcus returned her scrutiny, a little smile playing about his sensuous lips, telling Hayley that he was remembering too.

She sighed. It was all so idyllic that she had difficulty believing it wasn't some kind of lucid daydream, knowing it wasn't, because she could never have dreamed of anything as perfect as this.

She said drowsily, 'Marcus, how long is it since you did this kind of thing?'

His smile widened. 'Do you mean rowing on the river, with a girl?' He wrinkled his brow to remember. 'Not since my college days, probably.'

Hayley frowned. 'I meant rowing on the river, not necessarily with a girl. Was there always a girl?'

'Probably.' There was a teasing light in his vividly blue eyes.

As Hayley's frown deepened, he laughed. 'It was so long ago that I can't remember.'

'The experience, or the girls?' Even to her own ears, her voice sounded waspish. 'And why haven't you done it since college?'

He stopped rowing, resting the oars, leaning forward to touch her chin with a playful finger.

She jerked her head back irritably.

'Now who's got green eyes?'

She coloured. 'I'm not jealous. Just interested.'

'Actually, it's not very interesting. Believe it or not, there weren't that many girls then. I was too busy studying to take romance seriously.' He raised his brows sardonically. 'And since then, there's been no girl I've wanted to take rowing on the river.'

She made a mocking little sound. 'Not that any of them would have enjoyed it anyway, if Felicity is any sample of your taste.'

He shrugged amiably. 'I suppose not. Perhaps that's why I didn't take them.' He grinned into Hayley's still flushed face.

'Not even Felicity?' To her dismay she found she couldn't let the subject drop. 'She seems pretty special.'

His eyes narrowed on hers, with a glimmer of irritation in the blue depths. 'Yes, I suppose she is.' The glimmer sparked higher and seemed to issue a warning. 'Why not forget about the past and make the most of the present? Let's make this one day memorable.'

Hayley shivered as a cloud momentarily obscured the sun. One day. Was that all he was promising her? And after that? What then?

As the cloud moved on, unmasking the sun, she shook away her sudden melancholy, determined to enjoy the here and now and not waste it worrying about tomorrow.

His expression brightened, and Marcus leaned across to kiss her mouth briefly.

'I've got a surprise,' he said lightly. 'I persuaded the hotel to make up a hamper. What do you say we stop somewhere and eat?'

'That would be lovely.'

They picnicked on the bank, in the shade of the trees, eating fresh bread with chicken and cheese, crisp lettuce, firm red tomatoes and green apples. With the dramatic gesture of a magician pulling a rabbit from a hat, Marcus produced a bottle of champagne and two crystal glasses, after which everything seemed very mellow, the river and the countryside touched with sun-gold.

Later, after packing everything back into the little hamper, they sat on the car rug, Marcus with his back against the bole of a tree, and Hayley, sitting between his bent knees, resting against him, loving the feel of his hard chest behind her and the comfortable warmth of his arms clasped loosely about her waist.

Now and then she turned her face to him and they kissed—brief, sweet kisses that tingled through her body, too drowsy for passion. Her eyes were heavy, half closed against the light of the sun dappling through the branches, which swayed gently in the light breeze, the movement almost mesmeric. Once or twice the sun seemed to find a clear path through the shadows of the leaves and flashed in her eyes, transforming the world into a multi-coloured haze.

Perfect. Perfect. Perfect.

All too soon they were driving back to the hotel, their perfect day at an end. Hayley, like a miser hoarding against her bosom one last piece of treasure, clung to the anticipation of the night ahead.

They ate a wonderful dinner and afterwards danced out on the terrace to a small band playing discreetly in among the trees. Marcus held her easily, letting his body brush against hers in a tantalising promise. Hayley, goaded by the sweet torture, found herself growing alternately hot and cold, little shivers chasing along her nerves like music concerted by a master.

There was some kind of party going on, flash bulbs popping, people laughing, joking.

But Hayley registered little of what was going on around them, cocooned in the happiness of being in Marcus's arms on the tiny dance-floor.

She looked up at him, meeting the blue eyes, muted to pools of mystery by the dim moon and shaded lights.

It seemed incredible that this handsome, sophisticated man could be her lover, the first man—the only man—to steal behind her defences to her tender heart. Did he know, she wondered, that he was the first? And if he knew...did he care?

Almost as though in answer to her silent question, he drew her closer, pressing his lips against her hair, and she sighed, letting the sudden tension drain from her body.

'Hayley Morgan,' he murmured against the softness of her cheek, 'I want you now. Let's go.'

There was no time to ponder the brief flash of resentment before the excitement began, mounting swiftly to bring colour flooding to her cheeks.

Was their haste obvious? she wondered as she allowed him to take her hand and lead her off the small dance-floor, through the now crowded lounge, and on up the staircase to her room. Once inside, she was swept up into his arms, and nothing and no one mattered but this man who had the power to lift her to the heavens.

They made love through the night, and the first pearly fingers of dawn found them still in each other's arms.

As the car ate up the miles to the city, Hayley's heart began to sink. It had been a long and wonderful night, but now it was day, and Marcus had given her no hint of what lay ahead.

She stifled a yawn, and he turned with a warmly intimate smile that lifted her spirits.

'Tired?'

'A little.' She sighed. 'I don't know if I'll be up to much in the way of work today.'

He nodded. 'Which is why I'm taking you home. After all, it's Sunday, and since I intend to be out of the office anyway you may as well take the day to rest, sleep, whatever.'

Hayley was conscious of disappointment. At least in the office she stood a chance of seeing something of him. Left to herself at home, anticlimax was sure to set in.

Oh, why couldn't he just say something encouraging, loving... let her know what he was thinking? There had been no shortage of words between them last night, but not once had he mentioned love. Neither had she, for that matter. She'd been waiting for his lead, when she would have eagerly followed.

Many times the words, I love you, had trembled on her tongue, only to be swallowed back. He wanted her, and for that moment it had to be enough.

She gave a deep sigh, wishing she could ask him what she wanted to know. But there was an indefinable barrier between them this morning that spoke more clearly than words. He had promised her nothing... offered her nothing... but what had been between them.

She wouldn't spoil those memories now by asking for more.

Outside the flat he drew the car into the kerb, shutting off the engine. Hayley's heart leapt a little with hope. Did that mean he was coming in? Anthea would be with Lenny Barnes. They would have the flat to themselves.

'I won't stop,' he said, dashing the small flicker of hope. 'I have a few quite urgent personal matters to catch up on.'

She nodded, dismayed to find that tears were pressing behind her eyes. Oh, God, she wasn't going to cry, was she?

Swallowing hard, she said, her words sounding more like a plea than a statement, 'Then I'll see you in the office tomorrow.'

He raised his brows. 'Not before then? I thought we could have dinner together. I have some things to say to you.'

She said tentatively, over sudden palpitations, 'Good things, or bad?'

He took her hand in his and lifted it to his lips, pressing a kiss into her tingling palm.

'Wait and see. I'll come for you about eight.'

Hayley's heart sang as she climbed the stone steps to the front door. Later, soaking in a deep, warm bath, her mind kept wandering back to the last two days, reliving the highlights over and over until her head felt dizzy with the sweet visions.

And at eight o'clock tonight he would be here. He had things to say to her. She tried not to speculate on what those things would be. Too much anticipation often led to disappointment. It was better to wait and see.

The telephone was ringing as she wrapped herself in the large bath-towel. Still dripping, she was tempted to let it ring, but the thought that it might be Marcus had her stumbling out of the bathroom into the hall.

'Hayley! I wondered if you'd be home!' Anthea's strong voice rang in her ear. 'Have you seen the newspaper? I put it there on the hallstand.'

Hayley, who was struggling with her disappointment, said irritably, 'No, I haven't had time.' Then she added on a note of sarcasm, 'Why? Is there something I should be in a hurry to see?'

'Take a look for yourself.' Anthea made a wry sound. 'That must have been some meeting.'

Hayley demanded touchily, 'What do you mean by that?'

'Open the paper. You'll have a fit. And so will Marcus, I should think.'

With a sinking sensation in her stomach, Hayley wrapped the towel more securely around her and picked up the newspaper, skimming through the pages for something that would explain Anthea's obtuse remarks.

Turning another page, she found it and, as Anthea had predicted, her senses began to spin.

Headlines confronted her in large bold type: Maury's Most Promising Merger.

And underneath, a reported account that made her blood run cold.

Marcus Maury, currently involved in mergers with ailing engineering companies, found time this weekend for a little merging of his own. And who can blame him? Sexy secretary Hayley Morgan was the centre of a three-way tug of love, from which the tycoon emerged victorious. He was involved in a fracas with her former boss, who undoubtedly claimed prior rights.

Where did they get all their information from? Hayley wondered in amazement. Gripped with horror, she read on.

Felicity Braun, the beautiful British actress, who recently won the leading role in a new all-action American movie, is in for a big surprise. While she's busy wowing the boys across the Atlantic, her home-based male lead is taking time out for a little action of his own. Seems even she can't win them all!

The article continued in the same malicious vein, interspersed with photographs. One, which was obviously taken outside the hotel after the fight with Frank Heaton, showed her in Marcus's arms, with her face pressed against his throat and his hand stroking her hair. Further snaps showed her and Marcus kissing beneath the trees, dancing, and, finally, Marcus leading her up the hotel stairs to bed.

All those photographs taken—when and how? she wondered bemusedly. Eyes and cameras had been watching all the time. How could they not have noticed...been so oblivious?

With nausea tugging at her insides, Hayley flung down the paper and rushed for the bathroom.

She emerged minutes later, pale and dazed, to answer the telephone, which was ringing again insistently.

'Hayley.' Marcus's voice reached her through her haze. 'I'm just ringing to say I won't be able to make it to-night. Something important's cropped up.'

She said, in a nervous rush, 'I've just seen the paper.'

'Oh! Then you know.' He sounded bone-weary.

On the verge of tears, she gave a little hiccup. 'Oh, God, Marcus! I'm so sorry! What are we going to do?'

'You've nothing to be sorry for. And it's for me to do what's necessary,' he said abruptly. 'But it's a mess, nevertheless, and it's going to take some sorting out.' His tone told her he was keeping a tight rein on his fury.

'I'm coming into the office tomorrow,' she said insistently. 'If I stay at home I'll go mad.'

He sighed. 'OK, if that's what you want. You could start work on the notes you've taken.'

She said, sounding a little desperate, 'Will I see you there?'

'Not tomorrow, but soon.' His voice seemed distant. 'If any reporters come around, just stay calm and tell them nothing. Goodbye for now.'

He was going to ring off, she thought, in the grip of sudden panic.

'Marcus! Wait, please!'

His voice softened a little. 'I have to go, Hayley. I'll be in touch.'

He'd promised to keep in touch, but three days later there'd been no communication from him other than a curt message, taken by Anthea while Hayley was sleeping, to say he'd had to go out of town.

'Why didn't you wake me?' she demanded furiously. 'What did he mean? Out of town? Did he say where? Or when he'd be back?'

Anthea shook her head. 'No, I'm afraid not. He sounded fed up, and I didn't like to ask.'

Then, as Hayley's face crumpled, she gripped her in a fierce hug, patting her back in a clumsy gesture of comfort.

'Come on, Hay! He's not the only man in the world. You'll just have to forget him.'

Hayley tried to gulp back her tears. 'So you think he's giving me the brush-off too!'

'Probably. In his position you can hardly blame him.'

'You think not?' Hayley blazed. 'Just another boss playing around with his secretary, until the going gets rough?'

She sucked in her breath. Blame him! Did she blame him? No. Perhaps not. He was a man...like all men...like Frank Heaton and the rest. Just out for what he could get. Taking what she had so obviously put on a plate for him. Why should he refuse? How was he to know she hadn't really been aware of the name of the game?

But it had been so wonderful, so natural, so fulfilling. Could it have been that way if he'd had no feelings for her beyond lust? Perhaps it was possible for a man and what Anthea had hinted at was right: all he wanted now was to get out of the corner he found himself in.

But just to leave her like this, without a word of goodbye, cut like a knife, deep into her heart, because...despite everything she had hoped...

'Maybe this one's just for experience, Hay,' Anthea said softly.

Hayley wrenched herself away, unable to bear the confirmation in her friend's sympathetic eyes of her worst fears. If there ever had been a chance for her with Marcus, she'd lost it.

But the real confirmation, which left little room for doubt, came the following day, in the same paper, which headlined the news: Marcus Crosses the Atlantic to Confess. I've Been a Bad Boy!

'So that's what he meant by out of town,' she told herself, adding with bitter finality, 'And that's it! Finished! Kaput!' Before it had even had a chance to begin.

It seemed impossible that she could be hurt any more, until she saw a further heading the next day, above a photograph of Felicity in Marcus's arms: Marcus and Felicity Kiss and Make Up. Looks Like Wedding Bells.

Martin phoned to ask her out to lunch. She didn't feel like going, but he sounded so pleased with life that it would have been cruel to turn him down.

It was the first time she'd been outside the door in a week, the first time she'd made the least effort to hide the ravages of her unhappiness.

At Anthea's somewhat impatient insistence, she'd had her hair trimmed and set and was wearing the short-skirted black dress that Martin had admired.

Now she'd made the effort, she felt some of her spirit return. Anthea was right. Marcus Maury wasn't the only man in the world. There would be others. The difference was that in future she'd be the one in control.

And if her sore heart cried in bitter disbelief, she turned a determinedly deaf ear to its pain.

Martin, looking handsome and happy, met her at their agreed rendezvous with a gift of chocolates.

'I would have brought flowers too.' He grinned. 'But you'd have had to carry them around all day.'

Over the meal she asked him about his new job and enquired after Mr Heaton Senior.

'The job's great and the old man's blooming, now that he's got rid of that millstone of a son.'

'What's happened to Frank?' she asked, with an echo of the old familiar shudder the thought of him used to bring.

Martin grinned. 'Taken off for Australia, I believe. Just like the good old days, when villains got deported.'

Hayley groaned. 'Goodness help Australia.'

'I agree. But at least he's out of your hair how, for good. So you can relax.' He gave her a wry smile. 'I've got a message for you from Mr H. Any time you get fed up with being Maury's slave, there's a job waiting for you.'

Martin unexpectedly covered her hand with his, giving it a little squeeze that felt oddly comforting. 'He still thinks a lot of you, Hayley. And he's serious, if you should ever think of taking him up on it.'

When she got back to the office there were two men hanging about in the corridor.

'There she is,' one said, waving excitedly in Hayley's direction. 'Hello, darling! How about a picture?' He took her arm and pushed her against the wall. 'Put your hand on the handle of the door and move your head a little. At the moment it's obscuring his name, and we want that in.'

Hayley flung her arms up to hide her face as the bulb flashed.

'What are you doing here?' she demanded indignantly. 'No unauthorised person is allowed on this corridor.'

'Great!' the reporter said, undaunted. 'Get a shot of that expression, Fred. Even though he's gone chasing off after his old flame, the little secretary's loyal to the last. That defiant stance will knock them dead. Stick your boobs out a little bit——'

'Get out! Or I'll have you thrown out.' Hayley turned her back on them and fumbled her key into the lock. As the door gave, she rushed inside and slammed it tight shut against them.

'How about an exclusive story, darling?' the one persisted, his strident voice sounding through the thick door. 'How the great man used and abused his doting secretary. It will be worth a lot of money to you. Don't turn down a beautiful opportunity like this. Don't be a fool. He's not worth it.'

Hayley put her hands against her ears. Not worth it! The man's words echoed in her whirling brain. Perhaps he was right. Marcus himself had accused her of misplaced loyalty, and here she was again, lying at some great man's feet, waiting to be trampled on like any other doormat. It was no use to tell herself Marcus was different. He'd run off to make his peace with Felicity, leaving her here at the mercy of these hard-bitten reporters.

And maybe tomorrow he would be back, expecting her to have completed all the work of typing up the notes of the meetings. He would entrench himself behind the high wall of his authority and everything would go on, for him, just as it always had.

But for Hayley nothing would ever be the same again. She simply couldn't stay and go on pretending her heart wasn't broken.

Crossing to the desk in Marcus's room, she picked up the telephone. She dialled Security first and then she rang Martin.

CHAPTER ELEVEN

HAYLEY stood on the platform of the station patiently waiting for the train that would take her away from the heartache. Once she'd run away from Heaton's and escaped into the arms of a stranger. How could she have guessed then what would happen when strangers met? Now she was running back to Heaton's to escape a worse pain. Her brain was numb, her body stiff and aching, as though she'd taken a harsh beating. But her eyes were dry of tears. There was none left to shed.

In some deep, inner recess of her mind she knew that, when feeling eventually returned, she would be glad. It was finally over. Nothing more to hope for. When the dreams came now she would push them away—pack them tightly down into a compartment of her brain that she would label 'the past'.

She took a deep breath, letting the air, growing cool at the onset of autumn, pass deeply into her lungs, exhaling on a long drawn-out sigh. There was melancholy comfort in the realisation that it would soon be winter.

Then she could hibernate, cocoon her heart in the deepest ice until the spring, when hopefully the pain would have passed.

Turning her mind deliberately outwards, she scanned the platform. There were few people about at this early hour of a Monday morning, she noted with satisfaction, and the train drawing smoothly into the station was half empty. There would be plenty of room to find a solitary seat.

She found a corner seat to the rear of the train and settled down to stare desultorily out of the window as the train drew away. Her mind was turning inwards again, and she closed her eyes wearily.

It was no use now, trying to stem the misery. Everything reminded her of him. This was where it had all started...on a train. She'd kissed him and opened the door to the most wonderful—and the most hurtful—experiences of her life. How could she believe, for one moment, that the memories would ever leave her?

She was slipping into daydreams. Let them come. It was pointless to resist. She would welcome the pain and the pleasure.

He was near. She could sense his physical presence...almost believe he was here beside her. His lips were on hers, light, tender, tearing her heart from her body. His fingers were against her cheeks, brushing away the tears she made no attempt to stem.

'Hayley.'

He was whispering her name against her mouth, and her voice was husky as she replied.

'Marcus. Oh, Marcus.'

She shook herself awake, unable to bear any more, and found herself looking into the intense blue of his eyes—eyes that were guarded, uncertain.

'It really is you,' she whispered. 'I thought I was dreaming.'

His face softened. 'Was it a good dream?'

Reality was flooding back, and with it the barriers. There was no way she would lay herself open to him again.

'What are you doing here?' she demanded coldly.

He straightened, moving away from her in response to her withdrawal.

'Looking for a girl I met—a long time ago.'

She stared at him, wishing that her trembling weren't so obvious. 'Is that the only reason you're here?'

'The only reason,' he confirmed, his gaze never leaving her face.

There was something in his eyes, a kind of glimmer that longed to be a smile, but his expression was solemn, waiting.

'But then you've met so many girls, it's unlikely you'd remember one well enough to find her.'

'This one was special.' The corner of his mouth curved a little. 'A pushy little number, who kissed me without so much as a by-your-leave.'

There was no doubting now the warmth that was creeping into that vivid gaze. 'I'd like to pay her back.'

'You already have.' Hayley bit her lip in an effort to hide its trembling. 'A million times over.'

'Not nearly enough for all the aggravation I've suffered since she pushed her way into my life.' His hands gripped her shoulders. 'You probably won't appreciate the joke, my sweet Miss Pushy, but I've just got to kiss you again.'

Pulling her into his arms, he kissed her, his mouth hard and hungry, punishing her soft lips with a pain almost too joyous to bear.

When at last he lifted his head he looked down into her eyes, full of confusion and doubt, and groaned, burying his face in her neck and the thick scented tresses of her hair.

'Hayley. My God, how I've missed you.'

Their eyes met again, his full of a despairing tenderness, hers bright with new tears.

'Then why did you go away from me?'

'I didn't. Not for a moment. You were always there.'

Before she could absorb this strange reply he was kissing her again, his mouth warm and persuasive, leading her on and up, until she was soaring, her heart hammering a joyous beat against her ribs.

But some hint of sanity returned as his hands began to move against her. Flushed and breathless, she pushed him away.

'Marcus,' she hissed, 'this is not a bedroom. We're on a train, and this isn't an empty first-class compartment. There are people here.'

He pulled back and glanced around at the curious faces turned in their direction, but which looked hastily away on meeting his amused regard.

'Come on,' he said, pulling her to her feet. 'We're getting off at the next stop.'

'But Marcus,' she protested, 'I'll be late for the office. Mr Heaton——'

He pressed his mouth briefly against hers. 'Can find himself another secretary,' he said firmly. 'You belong to me.'

'But——'

'No buts.'

Marcus had hired a taxi, which had sped back to the city and deposited them outside his imposing flat. Paying the man off quickly, he ushered her inside and up the wide, immaculate staircase to his front door.

Even in her high state of excitement she couldn't help being impressed by the décor of his flat: the polished perfection of the wood, the deep, tasteful furnishings and rich, thick carpet, which combined to convey luxury with comfort on a scale she had never imagined, not like something out of a magazine, but an expression of his own personal taste that was exquisite.

'It's lovely,' she said faintly as they stood in the doorway to his living-room. 'Absolutely beautiful.'

'I agree,' he said, but he was looking at her face. 'Go and sit down and I'll bring you a cup of something. Tea or coffee?'

'Tea,' she said. But she wished that he'd stay with her instead of rushing off to the kitchen. There were so many questions racing through her mind.

As though he read her thoughts, he said, 'Questions and answers later.'

By the time he was back in the room and she was sipping her tea she'd become shy. In this setting he was, once again, very masculine and intimidating. This was his world and one she could only have imagined, but never coming near the reality.

Sensing her trepidation, he smiled.

'OK, where shall we begin?'

He was sitting some way from her in the corner curve of the settee. Hayley, stranded at the other end, felt suddenly lost. How could she reach him from here? How could she pour out her heart, laying it bare to him, when she still wasn't sure?

Gulping down the last of her tea, she waited. And when the silence and the waiting became unbearable she rushed in.

'How did you know where to find me?' There was a catch in her voice that revealed the depth of her pain.

'Anthea told me, when I rang this morning. You'd just left for the station.'

'I should have known I couldn't trust Anthea where you're concerned. She still thinks you're wonderful, in spite of everything.'

'But I've stopped being wonderful for you. Is that it?'

'Yes, that's it. I've learned some lessons about loyalty at last. It rarely works both ways. In your case, Felicity obviously came first. I couldn't stay on to find out where I fitted in.'

He shook his head. 'You should have waited, Hayley. I was coming back. But there were things to be done, and I didn't want you involved any more than was necessary. It could only have hurt you.'

'Do you think you rushing off to Felicity didn't hurt? So soon after everything we'd shared together? Did you even care?' Her jaw set stubbornly. 'No. Of course not! Your first thought was for Felicity. You went chasing off to her.'

'I went to Felicity, yes. For two reasons. One, to tell her, as kindly as possible, that it really was all over between us. I felt I had to do it face to face. I owed her that. We'd had a lot of good times.'

Hayley flinched. She didn't want to hear this—what she'd sensed all along—that he really did have feelings for the actress. 'And secondly?' she prompted.

'And secondly,' he repeated evenly, 'I wanted to draw the news hounds away from you, distract their attention to something they'd find more sensational, in the hope they'd leave you alone.'

'I see!' Her tone was ironic. 'You weren't worried about yourself?'

He shrugged. 'I've been through this sort of thing before. It leaves no mark on me. But you...' He grimaced. 'They'd have torn you to bits.'

She stared at him, wishing she could believe him. She longed for him... ached for him. But there was still so much standing between them.

'Did... did you make love to Felicity while you were there?' The whisper was barely audible.

'No. I haven't since the day I met you and sensed you'd brought something special into my life.'

'Then why did you propose marriage to her?'

His face hardened with genuine anger. 'That was paper talk, but you couldn't have known.'

'But you kissed her!' she insisted, close to tears. 'I saw the photograph.'

He nodded. 'Felicity and I are still friends. I was kissing a friend, not a lover.'

She made a disparaging sound. 'Do you mean there's a difference?'

He was suddenly angry. 'You tell me.'

With a sudden movement that caught her unawares he pulled her to him, his mouth devouring hers, his hard body trembling faintly, a fact that had her quaking in response. A heat began deep inside, rising quickly to overcome her.

With a groan of need she wrapped her arms about him, holding him as she had yearned to hold him for so long.

When at last he drew away from her, she was speechless.

He looked intently down at her, as though to confirm something to his satisfaction, and then hugged her to him, so that her face was buried in the hollow of his shoulder.

In a voice soft with laughter, he said, 'That's *not* how I kissed Felicity. Get the message?'

With her voice muffled against him, she said, 'Talking of messages, I have a confession to make. I forgot to give you a message from Felicity. The following day, after you'd taken me to dinner, she asked me to tell you she was sorry she hadn't been able to make it for dinner the night before, but she was free that evening.'

He pushed her away and tilted up her chin, looking with disturbing intensity into her eyes.

'And you believed her, of course? That you'd been second choice.'

She shrugged. 'It seemed likely.'

'Then how little you know me.' He smiled grimly. 'I asked you because I wanted you to have dinner with me.

I didn't ask Felicity. That was probably her way of getting back at you over the photograph of you and me out dining together.'

Hayley sighed, feeling a tight little knot in her heart dissolve. So it had been a lie after all.

'She was pretty horrible to me that day.'

'So you decided to get even by omitting to pass on her message to me?'

'Not consciously. But perhaps . . .' She bit her lip and drew her gaze from his. 'I'm sorry.'

'No hassle. I couldn't have made it anyway. We were booked to stay over that night, and I wasn't going to pass that up.' He gave her a sly grin. 'As a matter of fact, I knew about the message. I rang Felicity before we left to explain my absence on her last night in England. She told me she'd rung, though she didn't tell me the rest of it, and I half promised I'd combine some business with a visit to see her over there.'

'Which, of course, you did,' she said flatly.

'Yes,' he said, 'I did. And so now we can get down to another problem. You and me.'

She looked up at him tentatively. 'What about you and me?'

He shook his head. 'Well, for one thing, your letter of resignation has left me without a secretary at a very awkward time.' He pursed his lips thoughtfully. 'Although I suppose Audrey might manage what's left, now all the leg work's done.'

Hayley was flooded with disappointment. How quickly he could move from the personal to the impersonal.

'She'd never be able to translate my shorthand,' she said indignantly. 'What's stopping you from tearing up my resignation?'

He shook his head. 'I don't think I want to do that.'

Hayley looked outraged. 'Do you mean you'd rather have Audrey?'

'In my office? Yes. She's far less disruptive to the working routine. With you around all day, I've found it hard to think of anything other than how much I wanted you.'

'It wasn't obvious,' she said coolly. 'And I notice you said "wanted" not loved.'

'Loved... Wanted... Where you're concerned, it means the same to me. I can't love you without wanting you, nor want you without loving you. I've told you that countless times.'

'Never once,' she denied hotly, and then understood. With his arms and his lips, and his whole being, he'd said it. In her fear and uncertainty she had never heard. 'If only I'd known. I just couldn't believe ...'

He smiled, a curving movement of his lips that had her pulses racing. He was so gorgeous ... so desirable ...

'Looks as if we both had the same trouble. I couldn't believe you loved me the way I loved you ... the way your body told me you did.' He shook his head. 'Which is partly why I couldn't bring myself to commit myself to my feelings.'

'Partly?' Hayley felt breathless. There had been another barrier. She'd felt it.

'I have things to do, Hayley,' he said with a crease of worry between his brows. 'Things that will take up a lot of my time——'

She put her fingers against his lips. 'I knew about that before you did. You have an ambition to fulfil, for your grandfather as much as for yourself. I understand. But wouldn't it be easier to achieve if you had someone you love and who loves you to work for as well?'

He held her hand against his lips, kissing the palm and then each fingertip in turn, making her insides do all kinds of strange, delicious things.

'Perhaps. If it was the right woman. I just never thought I'd find one that understanding. Which is why

I always chose women with their own careers to follow . . . women who wouldn't really need me . . . except to fill the obvious gaps . . .'

'Women like Felicity?' she said softly.

'Like Felicity, yes,' he said a little defensively. 'But, unlike some of the others, she had a heart too. Which is why . . . if you hadn't come pushing into my life . . . I might have . . .' He shook his head slowly from side to side. 'Oh, Hayley, my sweet! You deserve so much and there is only so much time. What's left might not be enough.'

She shushed him. 'More than enough. So long as it's *all* that's left.' She shot him a coy glance. 'Besides, I may not have that much spare time myself. The large family I'm planning will probably take up a fair amount.'

He frowned. 'Sounds like a vicious circle. The more children we produce, the harder I'll have to work to keep them.'

'Sounds like a good bargain to me. Especially when you consider the fun we'll have producing those children.' Her eyes danced and then brimmed suddenly. 'Oh, Marcus! You'll never know how much I've wanted you. So much. *So* much.' A wayward tear slid down her cheek.

He brushed it away. 'We've wasted so much time.' His voice was suddenly light, and his eyes were smiling. 'We're going to have a heck of a job making it up. What do you say we get started?'

'Yes, please.' She snuggled deeper into his arms.

'Not here,' he said, sounding suddenly urgent. 'What I have in mind could be quite exhausting. I think the bedroom . . .'

He was bending to sweep her up in his arms when she remembered.

She said wistfully, 'I'm going to miss the office. Couldn't I carry on until——?'

He dumped her unceremoniously on the bed and began to undress.

'One thing at a time. Right now, I'm interviewing for a wife. And I warn you I exact the highest standards. In every department.'

Hayley choked with indignation. 'What a terrible proposal. If that's what it is.'

'It could be. Do you want the job?'

Outraged, she said, 'Yes, I do, but——'

'Then you've got it. We'll get married.'

She dissolved into giggles. 'But don't you want to see my curriculum vitae first?'

The laughter caught in her throat as she realised he was stark naked, towering above her.

'Of course.' He sat down on the bed and began undoing the buttons of her blouse, a smoky look in his blue eyes. 'We'll go through it together, bit by bit. Starting now.'

He was brushing the soft material from her shoulders, unhooking her bra to reveal the hard swell of her breasts. His hands reached out gently to touch her.

'A1 so far,' he said, but the teasing note was gone. This was suddenly no game.

He tugged at the zip of her skirt, and Hayley gasped at the intensity of his expression as, the last of her clothes removed, she lay naked before him. 'God, Hayley, it's new every time.'

Opening her arms to him, she said softly, 'Marcus, please. I've waited so long.'

He was beside her, his hard, muscular body crushed against hers.

'Oh, darling!' she murmured huskily as he looked deep into her eyes. 'I love you.'

'My little love.' His mouth covered hers in a long, arousing kiss, his hands against her soft skin, burning paths of fire that threatened to consume her.

But she held back, waiting, until she could bear it no longer.

'Say it, Marcus, please.'

'I love you,' he murmured softly, and kissed her again.

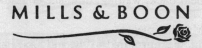

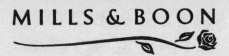

MILLS & BOON

HEARTS OF FIRE by Miranda Lee

Welcome to our compelling family saga set in the glamorous world of opal dealing in Australia. Laden with dark secrets, forbidden desires and scandalous discoveries, **Hearts of Fire** unfolds over a series of 6 books, but each book also features a passionate romance with a happy ending and can be read independently.

Book 1: SEDUCTION & SACRIFICE
Published: April 1994   *FREE* with Book 2

WATCH OUT for special promotions!

Lenore had loved Zachary Marsden secretly for years. Loyal, handsome and protective, Zachary was the perfect husband. Only Zachary would never leave his wife…would he?

Book 2: DESIRE & DECEPTION
Published: April 1994   Price £2.50

Jade had a name for Kyle Armstrong: *Mr Cool*. He was the new marketing manager at Whitmore Opals—the job *she* coveted. However, the more she tried to hate this usurper, the more she found him attractive…

Book 3: PASSION & THE PAST
Published: May 1994   Price £2.50

Melanie was intensely attracted to Royce Grantham—which shocked her! She'd been so sure after the tragic end of her marriage that she would never feel for any man again. How strong was her resolve not to repeat past mistakes?

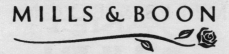

MILLS & BOON

HEARTS OF FIRE by Miranda Lee

Book 4: FANTASIES & THE FUTURE

Published: June 1994   Price £2.50

The man who came to mow the lawns was more stunning than any of Ava's fantasies, though she realised that Vincent Morelli thought she was just another rich, lonely housewife looking for excitement! But, Ava knew that her narrow, boring existence was gone forever…

Book 5: SCANDALS & SECRETS

Published: July 1994   Price £2.50

Celeste Campbell had lived on her hatred of Byron Whitmore for twenty years. Revenge was sweet…until news reached her that Byron was considering remarriage. Suddenly she found she could no longer deny all those long-buried feelings for him…

Book 6: MARRIAGE & MIRACLES

Published: August 1994   Price £2.50

Gemma's relationship with Nathan was in tatters, but her love for him remained intact—she was going to win him back! Gemma knew that Nathan's terrible past had turned his heart to stone, and she was asking for a miracle. But it was possible that one could happen, wasn't it?

Don't miss all six books!

HEART ⓣⓞ HEART

Win a year's supply of Romances
ABSOLUTELY FREE?

Yes, you can win one whole year's supply of Mills & Boon Romances. It's easy! Find a path through the maze, starting at the top left square and finishing at the bottom right.
The symbols must follow the sequence above.
You can move up, down, left, right and diagonally.

Please turn over for entry details

HEART ⟨TO⟩ HEART

SEND YOUR ENTRY NOW!

The first five correct entries picked out of the bag
after the closing date will each win one year's supply
of Mills & Boon Romances (six books every month for
twelve months - worth over £85).
What could be easier?

Don't forget to enter your
name and address in the
space below then put this
page in an envelope and
post it today (you don't
need a stamp).
Competition closes
31st November 1994.

HEART TO HEART Competition
FREEPOST
P.O. Box 236
Croydon
Surrey CR9 9EL

Are you a Reader Service subscriber?   Yes ☐   No ☐

Ms/Mrs/Miss/Mr _____ COMHH

Address _____

_____

_____

Postcode

Signature _____

One application per household. Offer valid only in U.K. and
Eire. You may be mailed with offers from other reputable
companies as a result of this application. Please tick
box if you would prefer not to receive such offers. ☐